TREASURE ISLAND

by Ken Ludwig

from the novel by
Robert Louis Stevenson

SAMUELFRENCH.COM

ISBN   978-0-573-65098-7   Printed in U.S.A.   #22958

IMPORTANT BILLING AND CREDIT REQUIREMENTS

All producers of *TREASURE ISLAND must* give credit to the Author of the Play in all programs distributed in connection with performances of the Play, and in all instances in which the title of the Play appears for the purposes of advertising, publicizing or otherwise exploiting the Play and /or a production. The name of the Author *must* appear on a separate line on which no other name appears, as shown below, and *must* appear in size of type not less than seventy-five percent of the size of the title type.

TREASURE ISLAND (100%)
by Ken Ludwig (75%)
Adapted from the novel by Robert Louis Stevenson (50%)

In addition the following credit *must* be given in all programs and publicity information distributed in association with this piece:

Originally commissioned and the World Premiere of "Treasure Island"
Produced by the Alley Theatre
Gregory Boyd, Artistic Director & Dean R. Gladden, Managing Director

Treasure Island had it's world premiere at the Alley Theatre, Gregory Boyd, Artistic Director, Dean R. Gladden Managing Director, on May 18th, 2007. The Scenic Designer was Eugene Lee, the Costume Designer was Constance Hoffman, the Lighting Designer was Clifton Taylor and the Original Music and Sound Design were by John Gromada. The Stage Managers were Elizabeth M. Berther and Terry Cranshaw. The production was under the direction of Gregory Boyd with the following cast:

JEMMY RATHBONE	Noble Shropshire
BLACK DOG	Jeffrey Bean
ISRAEL HANDS	John Tyson
EZEKIELHAZARD	Chris Hutchison
JOB O'BRIEN	James Belcher
JUSTICE DEATH	David Rainey
GEORGE MERRY	Mark Shanahan
CAPTAIN FLINT	John Feltch
JIM HAWKINS	Elizabeth Bunch
JIM'S MOTHER	Melissa Pritchett
THE BAILIFF	James Belcher
REVEREND MAINWARING	Noble Shropshire
TOWN DRUNK	James Black
DR. LIVESEY	John Feltch
BOY WITH BARROW	Chris Hutchison
BILLY BONES	Charles Krohn
BLIND PEW	John Tyson
SQUIRE TRELAWNEY	James Belcher
A CUT PURSE	Chris Hutchison
JOSIAH BLAND	Noble Shropshire
LONG JOHN SILVER	James Black
TOM MORGAN	Chris Hutchison
CAPTAIN SMOLLET	Jeffrey Bean
BEN GUNN	Noble Shropshire

PLACE AND TIME

The action takes place in England and the West Indies.
The time is 1774

CAST

Jim Hawkins		*Actor One*
Long John Silver		*Actor Two*
Jim's Father		

The Civilians	**The Pirates**	
Dr. Livesey	Captain Flint	*Actor Three*
Squire Trelawney	Job O'Brien	*Actor Four*
The Bailiff		
Captain Smollet	Black Dog	*Actor Five*
Reverend Mainwaring	Jemmy Rathbone	*Actor Six*
	Ben Gunn	
	Josiah Bland	
Jim's Mother	Anne Bonny	*Actor Seven*
Widow Drews	Justice Death	*Actor Eight*
Bailiff's son	Blind Pew	*Actor Nine*
Israel Hands	Calico Jack	
Bailiff's Son	George Merry	*Actor Ten*
Inn Guest	Ezekiel Hazard	*Actor Eleven*
Boy with Barrow	Tom Morgan	
	Cut Purse	
Bristol Sailor	Billy Bones	*Actor Twelve*

Additional Pirates as needed

In addition, everyone except Jim Hawkins and Long John Silver doubles, variously, as the customers at the Admiral Benbow Inn, the sailors in Bristol, a lady at the dock, etc.

AUTHOR'S NOTE

In the world premiere production of my adaptation of Treasure Island, Jim Hawkins was played by a woman. This was my intention when I wrote the piece because it seemed to me at the time that the best way to find an actor who can play a 14-year-old boy who, in the course of the play, experiences the adventure of a lifetime, is to cast a woman of 20 or 30 who has enough acting experience to really knock the socks off such an enormously demanding role.

However, I can also well imagine the role being played by the right young man, in which case the play would grow in other directions and preserve different aspects of Stevenson's tale of boyhood. In England, in particular, there may be dangers in casting an actress as Jim, as it might suggest Pantomime, which is not, of course, the world of this play. Indeed, as I write this Note, a West End production of the play is being planned for London and we'll probably cast a boy as Jim. All in all, future producers should feel free to cast the play as they see fit.

Regardless of casting, it seems to me that the key to understanding Treasure Island is to recognize that the story created by Stevenson is not just a swashbuckler, though it certainly is that. It is primarily a story of the heart; a story about a boy growing up; and a story about all of us finding out who we are. The relationship between Jim Hawkins and John Silver as created by Stevenson (I take no credit) is a love story of genuine emotional depth. We care about these complex souls from the moment we meet them, and we watch their relationship grow with an almost breathless sense of anticipation. Will they become friends or foes? Will Silver ever be honest with Jim? And will Jim ever forgive the old rogue and admit him back into the shadows of his heart?

As a lover of Shakespeare, I was delighted to discover while writing this adaptation that while Stevenson never makes Shakespeare explicit in his novel, Treasure Island is infused with Shakespeare from beginning to end. I find this in everything from the poise of the plotting to the power of the characters; from the drama of the scene structure to the richness of the language. The narrative voice that Jim assumes in the novel has some of the same clear-eyed lushness that we hear in Shakespeare's middle voice, in plays like As You Like It and Twelfth Night, Henry V and Julius Caesar. Moreover, Jim's boyish jauntiness reminds me of Rosalind and Viola, two characters who also go on voyages of self-discovery, both of them women dressed as men who, once upon a time, were played by boy actors. I tried to highlight these Shakespearean themes by emphasizing Jim's devotion to his father, and making the elder Hawkins into a man who loved his son so much that he spent hours every week teaching him to recite Shakespeare by the page-full. (I've spent the past several years teaching my own children large swaths of Shakespeare, so I cannot claim disinterest here.)

Also by way of casting: I believe that the play can hold as many pirates as the producer can find. So if a particular production has the luxury of a large cast, please feel free to eliminate the doubling that I outline on the casting page. The goal of the production should be wild, rollicking, frightening, breathless and moving. Any means to that end should be embraced – and if that means more actors and more pirates, then all the better. Equally, if it means fewer actors and even more doubling than I suggest on the casting page – and if the director is ingenious enough to figure out how to do it – then I'm all for that as well. Large cast or small, it's all a matter of preserving the spirit of the piece.

Finally, for me, one of the marvels of Treasure Island is that virtually all of the characters that Stevenson created in the book are flamboyantly larger than life. Pew is the epitome of evil, just as Bones is the quintessence of frightened bravado. Livesy is the stalwart friend we all dream of having, while Trelawney is a loveable booby. Jim is all eagerness and boyish joy, just as Silver has the heart of a hero and the ruthless cunning of a politician. These are roles made in heaven – or the heaven created by Stevenson's pen – and the play is meant to glitter with the gold of their inner lights.

A NOTE ON THE PARROT

There's an old saying in show business suggesting that you should always avoid working with children and animals. There are no children in this play, but there is, unavoidably, a parrot because he was just too famous to leave out.

But please be warned! When producing this play, you must be careful that the parrot doesn't seem prominent or silly in any way. He shouldn't provoke laughs. Ever. He should be neutral. In the world premiere production of the play at the Alley Theatre we thought we had the perfect parrot: he was an exact reproduction of a real parrot, the right size, the right colors, with a real parrot's voice; but in the previews he got giggles from the audience. The solution was to have him appear in a cage (as indicated in the stage directions) and, whenever he had to be onstage, to have the cage placed in the shadows at the side of the stage where the parrot could barely be glimpsed. It was the only way we could prevent the audience from responding in the wrong way, and I highly recommend it. Otherwise the parrot will upstage everybody in the scene. And while the parrot may enjoy it, the rest of us won't. Many thanks.

Ken Ludwig

January 13, 2008

"O'er the glad waters of the dark blue sea,
Our thoughts as boundless, and our souls as free,
Far as the breeze can bear, the billows foam,
Survey our empire, and behold our home!"

Such were the notes that from the Pirate's isle
Around the kindling watch-fire rang the while;
Such were the sounds that thrill'd the rocks along,
And unto ears as rugged seem'd a song!

*   *   *

He left a Corsair's name to other times,
Link'd with one virtue, and a thousand crimes.

The Corsair, Lord Byron

For my two swashbucklers, Olivia and Jack.

ACT I
Scene 1

(Strong music attacks us in the darkness. Prokofiev, here and throughout the play. Then the lights come up on a pirate ship in 1774 in the middle of a desperate chase across the deck. The ship is rolling, as mighty waves slap the side of the vessel without mercy. Lightning flashes and thunder roars, as though the gods were playing roughly with their favorite toys. "As flies to wanton boys, are we to the gods? They kill us for their sport." Everything about this moment is dangerous and exciting.
The man being chased is named JEMMY RATHBONE. He's sly and filthy. The pirates chasing him include ISRAEL HANDS, BLACK DOG, ANNE BONNY, GEORGE MERRY, EZEKIEL HAZARD, JOB O'BRIEN and JUSTICE DEATH. With shouts and cries, they careen around the deck, in and out of the foc'sle, around the bowsprit and through the rigging. These pirates are after blood.)

HANDS.
Grab 'im!
    DEATH.

              'old 'im!

11

HANDS.

Trap 'im between you, ya dogs!

MERRY.

You miserable dolts! How far can he get?!
We're on a Ship!

BONNY.

I got him!

BLACK DOG.

Got him!

RATHBONE.

(Caught)

Ahhhhhhhhhhhhhhhhhh!

(The pirates tackle him and pin his arms behind him.)

BLACK DOG.

Bonny, hold him down!

BONNY.

Stop yer squirmin!

RATHBONE.

I ain't done nothin'!

Leave me alone!

MERRY.

Get up, you dog!

BLACK DOG.

Where is it?!

RATHBONE.

I never seen it!

HAZARD.

You lyin' filth, *where is it!*

RATHBONE.

Get Flint! He'll tell ya it ain't me!
Cap'n Flint!!!

    BONNY.

    I wouldn't do that if I was you.

    RATHBONE.

(In tears, knowing he's about to be killed.)
I never seen it in me life, I swear!
FLINT! FOR GOD'S SAKE! COME OUT HERE!
FLIIIIIINT!

    HANDS.

Here he comes!

    BONNY.

        It's Flint.

    DEATH.

                             Flint.

    BLACK DOG.

                           It's Flint!

    MERRY.

Get outa the way!

(CAPTAIN JAMES FLINT steps out of the foc'sle. He looks evil beyond description. He has a hideous scar on one side of his face. He has a mop of greasy red hair sticking out of the sides of his black, tattered hat. He's missing three fingers from his left hand. And he hasn't shaved in a week. He carries himself, however, with some daintiness, and he uses the fingers he has left to him with the delicacy that civilized people use to pick up fine jewelry or canapés.)

RATHBONE.

Oh, Cap'n Flint! Thank God above you's 'ere.
They was gonna kill me, Cap'n. Kill me fer
nothin'!

*(GEORGE MERRY brings his cutlass down towards
RATHBONE'S head and CAPTAIN FLINT parries the blow
with a flick of his wrist, saving RATHBONE'S life. Then, to
RATHBONE:)*

FLINT.

Where…is…the map?

RATHBONE.

Map, sir?

FLINT.

Little piece o' paper with lines on it.

RATHBONE.

I ain't got it, Cap'n. I never seen it.

FLINT.

Think very hard about this, Jemmy.

RATHBONE.

I swear to you on me life, sir!

FLINT.

"Your life?" Well that's a very appropriate
choice of language, now ain't it, Jemmy?
(To Death – and meaning it.)
Skin him alive.

(They drag RATHBONE away.)

RATHBONE.

Nooooooooooooo!

FLINT.

*Tear the
Flesh from his bones, cut out his heart through his
Throat and throw the whole mess overboard!!*

RATHBONE.

Sir I swear, I ain't got the map!

FLINT.

Who's got it then?

RATHBONE.

…Billy Bones, sir.

BONNY.

But Bones is dead.

RATHBONE.

No he ain't. Ya thought he was dead, we all did.
But that night after the treasure was buried
And the men what buried it put to death,
Well I was watch that night and around about
Three bells I hears a noise, and afore I knows it
There comes Billy Bones a-clamberin' over
The side o' the ship – 'e 'ad survived, ya see –
And he limps to your quarters and he steals the map!

FLINT.

Bones does?

RATHBONE.

And then I-I stops him like, right here on this deck,
And I says "Give me the map! That there belongs to
Captain Flint, the very man what gave me
Me start in this most noble o' professions."
'Cause it's like I worships you, Cap'n. You're my
Hero like.

FLINT.

And Bones?

RATHBONE.

(In tears.)

He threatens me, and says that if I ever
Says a word about it, then he'll track
Me down and kill me. And then he was over the side
Like that!

FLINT.

I see, I see.

And you didn't plan to meet up with him
Later and divide the spoils, now did ya?
All private like? Between old friends?

RATHBONE.

No, sir! The map is yours, sir! Like I said!

FLINT.

You're a good boy, Jemmy.

RATHBONE.

(Relieved)

Thank you, sir.

FLINT.

But you're a liar!

(Whap! FLINT strikes RATHBONE across the face so hard that it brings RATHBONE to his knees.)

You were going to split it with him!

(Whap!)

And Bones is alive and he's got the *map!*

(Whap!)

Boys, kill him.

(The PIRATES grab him.)

RATHBONE.

Ahhh!

BONNY.

String him up!

DEATH.

Cut him to pieces!

MERRY.

Drownd him!

FLINT.

Oh just throw him overboard and be done with it!

RATHBONE.

Noooooooooooooooooooo!

(As the PIRATES drag him toward the side of the ship, RATHBONE struggles with all his might. Suddenly, he gets away from them, grabbing a cutlass as he goes. He rushes straight for FLINT, who has turned his back on the proceedings –

– and plunges the blade deep into FLINT'S back.

FLINT cries out and falls to the deck. RATHBONE turns to face the other pirates.)

RATHBONE.

Stay back! Boys. Please. I done it for all of us.

MERRY.

(Approaching RATHBONE.)

Kill 'im!

BONNY.

Kill 'im!

BLACK DOG.

Kill 'im!

HANDS.

Kill 'im!

ALL THE PIRATES.

KILL 'IM!

RATHBONE.
Pleeeeeeeeeeease!

(The lights fade quickly and are out by the time the PIRATES reach him. With a crack of thunder, the scene ends and...)

Scene 2

(JIM HAWKINS appears. He's a boy of 14, wiser and graver than his years imply. He could well be played by a woman. As he speaks to us, the Admiral Benbow Inn forms behind him.)

JIM. I remember it all as though it were yesterday. The adventure of my life, that changed me from a boy to a man and is still changing me and will never stop. It began in the spring of 1775 and I, but 14 years old, was in charge of the family business, the Admiral Benbow Inn on Black Hill Cove on the south coast of England. I remember the date, for that was the year my poor dear father died, a blow from which I will never recover. It was during this illness that he went to London to find a specialist who might save him.

FATHER. "The doctors are better there, Jim. I'll get through this, I promise. And so will you."

JIM. "Please take me with you, Father! Please! *Please!*" I begged him day and night, but he wouldn't do it. Looking back, I can see that he was protecting me.

FATHER. "Take care of your mother, son. She needs you now."

JIM. "Yes, Father. I promise." A letter reached us, three months later, that he died in London – in that faceless city, alone and without his son. Here was the man I worshipped, ate with, slept with, laughed with; taken from me in a single instant, in the time it takes a beam of sunlight to disappear over the farthest hill. Farthest. Farther. Father. Gone. While he was alive, we went everywhere together, coupled and inseparable, like Juno's swans. If that sounds Shakespearean, it is. My father was a simple man, but he loved reciting Shakespeare, which he'd studied as a boy. He kept a copy with him in the left-hand pocket of his jacket, and he taught me speeches from the great plays as we tramped the downs together, braced against the icy cold. "Friends, Romans, countrymen!" he roared against the wind; and I shouted back: "Lend me your ears!" and we'd laugh together and on we'd go, line after line, mile after mile. My best friend. Soon gone. Ever loved. So it was, in the year he died, that my mother said.

MOTHER. "You're a man now Jim. I believe I can run the inn without your father, but I'll need your help."

JIM. "Of course, Mother. And I promise that you'll never want for anything as long as I'm alive." Bold words, but from the heart. And so we picked up the reins of the business and kept it pulling like an ailing dray as best we could. *(And now the inn comes to life behind JIM.)* Customers came, village folk, Old Widow Drews, who lost her astonished husband to the sea; the bailiff and his two sons, one good, the other not; the Reverend Mainwaring, who stood next to me at my father's funeral and held my hand; and Dr. Livesy, the physician who ministered to my father in those months before his untimely death; – and all the while, I delivered pints of ale and kept the tables clean and collected the bills, looking the other way when money was tight for this or that one; so on we rode, filling our lives with everything in existence that was routine and commonplace – until the day the pirate arrived.

(BILLY BONES appears on the horizon, approaching the inn. He's a tall, strong, heavy, nut-brown man; his tarry pigtail falling over the shoulders of his soiled blue coat; his hands ragged and scarred, with black, broken nails; and a saber cut across one cheek, a dirty, livid white. He's followed by a boy pushing a hand barrow, and on the barrow is a seaman's chest.)

    BONES.
(Singing)
FIFTEEN MEN ON A DEAD MAN'S CHEST –
YO-HO-HO AND A BOTTLE OF RUM!
DRINK AND THE DEVIL HAD DONE FOR THE REST –
YO-HO-HO AND A BOTTLE OF RUM!
(To JIM.)
You! Boy! What's yer name?!

    JIM. Jim Hawkins, sir.

    BONES. Tell me, Jim Hawkinsir, d'ye get much company in this here grog shop o' yourn?

    JIM. Very little, sir. The nearest town is some four miles off.

    BONES. That's just what I was hopin' you'd say. Now move me in. I'll take that room up there with the pretty view o' the cove and the road. *(To the boy pushing the hand barrow:)*

You! Take the chest indoors! Shake a leg! And if ya even *think* of takin' a little peeky like inside that chest when I ain't lookin', I'll reach down yer throat and cut yer gizzard out!

BOY. Yes, Cap'n!

BONES. Now listen to me, Jim Hawkinsir. I need yer help.

JIM. My help?

BONES. I want you to keep a weather eye open for a seafarin' man with one leg. And you let me know the moment he shows himself. D'ya understand?

JIM. Yes sir. Is he a friend of yours?

BONES. Friend? The man is a friend to no livin' creature, and if he ever turns his back on ya – ya shoot him till you're sure he's dead and pray his ghost don't hunt ya down. You savvy?

JIM. Yes sir. *(To the audience.)* I need scarcely say how the one-legged man now haunted my dreams. On stormy nights, when the wind shook the four corners of the house, and the surf roared along the cove and up the cliffs, I would see him in a thousand forms, and with a thousand diabolical expressions. Now the leg would be cut off at the knee, now at the hip; now he was a monstrous kind of a creature who had six legs and scuttled over trees and houses like a giant spider, his face black and pointed like a beak. To see him thus leap and run and pursue me over the hedge and ditch of my own back yard was the worst of nightmares.

BONES. Hey! Stop yer daydreamin', boy, and get me some rum.

JIM. But it's breakfast time, sir.

BONES.
Rum, I say! *Now,* boy! And make it quick!
Rum! Rum! Rum! Rum!

Rum! Rum! Rum! Rum!

*(The chanting of "Rum!" sets up a musical ground as we move
     to the inside of the inn several weeks later.*
*We now see the regular customers of the ADMIRAL BENBOW,
     all at their tables, feeling put upon as BILLY BONES laughs
     heartily and sings to them.)*

JIM. There were nights at the inn when he took a deal more
rum than his head would carry; and he would call for glasses
round and force all the trembling company to bear a chorus to
his singing.

BONES.
"FIFTEEN MEN ON A DEAD MAN'S CHEST – "
Sing out, ya swabs! Lemme hear ya!

REVEREND   MAINWARING. *(Rising, timidly.)* I'm
afraid I do have to go now…

BONES. *SIT DOWN! ALL OF YA!* Jim Hawkinsir!
More rum fer the whole table!
There'll be no drinkin' alone at this here
Grog shop. Not while I'm still drawin'
Breath from me plaguey lungs.
Now raise yer voices to the God o' Drink
And lemme hear ya sing out this time!

(The customers join in feebly.)

BONES.
"FIFTEEN MEN ON A DEAD MAN'S CHEST,
YO-HO-HO AND A BOTTLE O' – !

(BONES notices that DR. LIVESY is talking quietly to the BAILIFF.)

BONES. You! Stop yer jabberin' and lemme hear ya sing!

DR. LIVESY. *(Coldly, not giving an inch.)* Are you addressing me, sir?

BONES. That I am!

DR. LIVESY. Then you are interrupting and I suggest you don't.

JIM. Dr. Livesy –

DR. LIVESY. And let me warn you, as a medical matter, that if you keep on drinking as much rum as you have tonight, the world will soon be quit of a very filthy scoundrel.

(BONES glares at LIVESY – then sweeps all the mugs off the table, and they go clattering onto the floor. In the same gesture, he pulls out a knife and snaps it open and holds it in front of LIVESY'S face.)

BONES. Arrrr!

DR. LIVESY. Put up that knife this instant, sir, or upon my honor you will hang by the neck at the next assizes. …And now I believe that my good neighbors here would like to go home for the night.

(Another silence, then BONES gives in, humiliated.)

BONES.
… Get out! Now! All o'ya! GOOOOOO!

(The customers scatter quickly and leave the inn. As they go,
DR. LIVESY confers quietly with JIM:)

DR. LIVESY. If you have any trouble with this scoundrel,
get someone to find me and I'll come right over.

JIM. Thank you, sir. I will.

BONES. *Out! Out! Out! (DR. LIVESY takes leave of JIM*
and goes, closing the door of the inn behind him, leaving JIM
alone with BONES.) Rum, boy! Get me some rum!

JIM. But sir, you heard what the doctor said.

BONES. Doctors is all swabs and what do they know
about seafarin' men. I been in places as hot as pitch and mates
droppin' round with Yellow Jack and I lived on rum. It's been
meat and drink and man and wife to me. So it's rum I say and
be quick about it! *(A knock at the door. BONES is angry at*
the interruption.) 'Swounds and blast it all! I'll wager it's that
Reverend's wife with her disapprovin' air, forgettin' her reticule
or somethin'…

(BONES opens the door – and BLACK DOG is standing in
the doorway. He's a pale, tallowy creature, wanting two
fingers of the left hand.)

BLACK DOG. Why hello, Billy boy. How's me old
swabber, eh?

(BONES gasps and staggers back.)

BONES. Black Dog ...

BLACK DOG. Ay, Black Dog as ever was, come to see his old shipmate Billy Bones at the "Admiral Benbow" inn.

BONES. Well speak up then. What d'ya want?

BLACK DOG. What do I want? What I want at the moment is a glass o' rum. And I wonder if this handsome young lad here would fetch it for me.

(JIM looks to BONES for his approval, and BONES nods.)

BONES. What else do ya want?

BLACK DOG. *(Turning nasty.)* What d'ya think I want, Bill? And why d'ya think we been trackin' you down over half o' southern England?

BONES. Go to the devil!

BLACK DOG. Go to the devil is it? And you the man that betrayed us, Bill, and stole the map.

BONES. It's a lie! Ya left me for dead! Ya tried to cut me outa the split and so I turned the tables on ya! *Now* you tells me that you didn't deserve it, eh? Hanh?! *IS THAT WHAT YOU'RE SAYIN'?!*

BLACK DOG. Bill, Bill, you're gettin' all excited. You'd think that somebody come here to kill you or somethin'.

BONES. Don't you threaten me, you villain.

BLACK DOG. Now who am I to threaten the great Billy Bones, second mate to Captain James Flint, may he rest in peace.

(He crosses himself.)

BONES. Flint's dead?

BLACK DOG. And won't we all remember his lovin' kindness while among us.

BONES. Who's Cap'n now?

BLACK DOG. Who do you think?

BONES. God a'mighty.

BLACK DOG. It's him what ordered yer execution, Bill. Pity he won't be with us tonight.

BONES. Dog, listen –

BLACK DOG. No, you listen to me, Billy Bones, cause you're as good as dead and you know it. Now you hand me the map, right now, and I'll tell 'em that you cooperated.

BONES. … All right, I'll do it. Only I got a little wrinkle to suggest. Come 'ere.

(BLACK DOG comes a little closer – and BILLY whips out his knife, grabs BLACK DOG around the neck and holds the knife at BLACK DOG'S throat, trembling with rage.)

BONES. The wrinkle is, you tell 'em that *nobody* threatens Billy Bones. That I can still beat the tar outa every one of 'em, and that I might – just might – consider joinin' up with me old mates, provided that you make me captain o' the crew as I been deservin' since Maddygascar! *Now you tell 'em all that, you savvy?!!*

(BLACK DOG shakes his head, gargling for air –)

BLACK DOG. Arghhhh.

(–and BONES pulls his arm even tighter around BLACK DOG'S neck.)

JIM. Sir, don't kill him – !

(BONES is distracted by JIM'S voice – and BLACK DOG seizes the moment to break away. He pulls his cutlass and BONES pulls his – and the two men fight, slashing away fiercely. After several passes, BONES lands a glancing blow on BLACK DOG'S distaff arm and BLACK DOG cries out with pain. Then BLACK DOG turns and runs out the door in full retreat. BONES rushes to the door and cries after him:)

BONES. Come back, ya coward! I'll split yer gizzard! I'll take yer arm off! I'll make ya wish you'd never been – *Ah!*

(He seizes his chest and drops to his knees. He's having a heart attack and is instantly incapacitated, gasping for air.)

JIM. *Mr. Bones!*
BONES. The dog, I should a' split 'im ...
JIM. What's the matter, sir?!
BONES. *(His voice strangled.)* I think it's me heart... finally playin' me the fool...
JIM. I'll fetch Doctor Livesy.
BONES. No! No need. I gotta get outa this place, and fast ...

(He staggers to the side of the room and pulls his sea chest out of hiding.)

JIM. Sir, what are you doing?!

BONES. The map! I gotta get it away from their clutches
...

*(BONES opens the chest and pours out clothing, a quadrant,
tobacco pouch, pipes, etc., then tears away the lining of
the lid to reveal a hidden section where the map has been
tucked away. As he does all this, he continues to talk:)*

BONES.
They'll send the blind man with the stick next.
Old Blind Pew, with the black spot. He's pure
Evil. Some think he's the horny Devil
Himself with cloven hooves in them shoes o' his.
He likes to work in the black o' night cause nobody
Else can see then neither. Here it is!

*(The map! BONES holds it up into the light and it almost glows
with mystery and danger.)*

JIM. Is it a...treasure map?
BONES.
(With awe.) Flint's map. The great Captain Flint.
And it's pointin' straight to hundreds o' thousands, boy,
Hundreds o' thousands in gold and silver and little
Trinkets made o' pearls. Now take it.
JIM. Me?
BONES. You'll be me eyes and legs, boy. You'll do the
findin' and we'll split it down the middle.
JIM. But I don't think that I'm the one to –
BONES. *Take it!!*

(JIM takes the map and gazes at it. As he starts to stuff it into his

*shirt, we hear "Tap tap...tap tap ..." – the sound of a blind
man's stick on the rocks outside the inn. The sound is faint
at first, then gets closer and closer. "Tap...tap tap...")*
JIM. ... Sir?
BONES. *Shhh!!!!*

("Tap tap...tap...tap tap...")

BONES. *(As though life itself is escaping from his lips.)*
Blind Pew!

*(The door opens with a creak. In the shadow of the doorway
is a small, hunched man out of a nightmare. He wears a
green eyeshade over his eyes and nose; he's stooped over,
as if with age or weakness; he wears a huge old tattered
sea-cloak with a hood that makes him look deformed; and
the hand that protrudes from the cloak and holds the stick
is gnarled and bent. He peers upward, plainly blind.
JIM and BONES stand stock still, and PEW doesn't know where
they are.)*

BLIND PEW.
Ah, light!
I feel the prickle of it on me
Skin as if there's daybreak lying ahead
And calling out to me like a nice warm fire.
Eh? Hanh? Now will any kind friend inform
A poor blind beggar man in just what part
Of this blessed land he be?

JIM. You're at the Admiral Benbow Inn, sir, Black Hill
Cove.

BLIND PEW.
Ah, now ain't that a sweet young voice before me.
A precious voice belonging to a precious lad.
I was a lad once too, ya know,
And had a father and a mother and a voice
As sweet as a ribbon of honey just like your own.
And I could climb to the top of puzzle trees
And play lookout on the beach with me friends –
The ones I had; or stay at home
All snug up in me father's woolly great coat
Gazing at the fire and dreaming of the
Dawning of the world and the creation of man.
Now will you give old Blind Pew your hand,
Me kind young friend, and lead me into this
Fine old house?

(JIM holds out his hand and the horrible, soft-spoken, eyeless
creature grabs it like a vise.)

    JIM. No! Leave go! *Ah!*

(JIM struggles to withdraw, but the blind man pulls him closer,
with a single, violent action of his shockingly powerful
arm.)

    BLIND PEW.
Now lead me in to Billy Bones young feller
Or I'll have to break your arm and do this to you.

(PEW wrenches JIM'S arm so hard that JIM cries out in intense
pain and almost faints.)

JIM. *AHHH!*
*(BILLY BONES reacts involuntarily, making a noise, and
   BLIND PEW whips around in his direction.)*

BLIND PEW.
Is that you, Bill? Eh? Of course it is,
Cause I can hear your heart beating against your chest.
Oh Bill, Bill, Bill, Bill, Bill,
Bill, Bill, we've missed you on the ship
Something terrible, aye, for who else did
The rats have to look up to after you left?
(BONES tries to move.)
Ah ah, just stay where you are. Don't even think
About moving yourself the width of an oak leaf.
I may be blind, but I can hear a finger stirring across the
Stretch of a galleon. Now put out your left hand.

*(BONES sits in fear and doesn't move. PEW starts chanting
   again.)*

Put out your left hand, put out your left hand,
Put out your left hand, put out your left hand,
Put out your left hand, *put it out I say!*
(BONES puts his hand out.)
Now, boy, take his left hand by the wrist
And bring it near to my right.
(JIM does as he's told.)
Now open your hand, my dear friend.
Open your hand my dear friend
Open your hand my dear friend
Open your hand my dear friend

Open your hand my dear friend
That's a boy!
Ooh, she's gettin' soft that old hand is,
Soft as the belly of a newborn kitten. Ohh…
*(He rubs the inside of BONES'S hand, almost erotically; and
    then he passes a piece of paper from the hollow of his
    own hand into that of BONES, then closes BONES'S hand
    around it. As he does it, he sighs with relief.)*

And now that's done. And I shall see you anon,
Billy Bones, in that glorious place where
The light gets shared between the just and the wicked.

*(He taps his way unerringly to the door. Then he grabs JIM and
    holds him close.)*

I wish I'd made your better acquaintance, young fella,
Cause I cotton strongly to the smell o' your hair.

*(He flings JIM away, and he's gone. JIM recovers and hurries
    over to BONES, who's in shock.)*

    JIM. What did he give you, sir?…Oh. It's only a piece of
paper.
    BONES. *(With horrible dread.)* The black spot. What does
it say, on t'other side?
    JIM. "Eight o'clock."
    BONES. And what time is it now?!
    JIM. Ten till eight.

(BONES gets agitated and struggles to his feet.)

BONES.
Ten minutes, boy, and then this place'll be
Swarmin' with pirates – Cap'n Flint's whole crew –
They'll tear the place apart and kill everything
That gets in their way, includin' you and me.
    JIM. But I've done nothing!
    BONES. They don't care! They want the map and they'll
stop at nothin' to get it.
    JIM. *(Calling) Mother! Quick! Come down!*
    BONES. They could be here in seconds!
    JIM. *Mother!*...I'll be right back.

(JIM dashes up the stairs to fetch his mother, leaving BONES
    alone. BONES starts talking to himself, getting more and
    more agitated by the second.)

BONES.
The dirty swabs. They won't stop Billy Bones,
They won't. Not in a month o' Sundays. Ha!
...Wait! I see 'em comin'!...
The whole pack of 'em, bearin' down on me!
You're all wearin' black, eh? Like the
Black spot itself – remindin' me o' the
Black deeds I done all me life?
Is that what you're about? Hanh? Shovin' the
Widows in me face, and the cryin' children
And the weepin' fathers? *Well ya know what?!*
I'll do no mournin' for the life I led, and no dyin' neither.
It ain't my care! It ain't my problem! It ain't
My responsi – argh!
(He clutches his heart in violent confusion.)
AAAARGHHHHH!

*(He falls over like a felled tree, landing with a thump, and lies
    still, as JIM and his mother appear on the stairs. JIM runs
    over to him and listens at his chest.)*

JIM. ... He's dead. ...Quick, Mother, we have to run.
MOTHER. Run?
JIM. Run, quickly! Pirates are coming! They'll tear the
house apart!
MOTHER. But why?!
JIM. There's no time to explain –!
MOTHER. But we can't just leave him.
JIM. We have to! Please! You'll have to trust me! Come
on!

*(They hurry to the door. JIM is just about to open the door,
    when he stops dead and doesn't move.)*

MOTHER. Jim?
JIM. *Shh!*

*(Silence. Then we hear "Tap ...tap tap... " JIM turns white. For
    a moment he doesn't know what to do. Then, as silently as
    possible, he pulls the beam of wood across the door that
    stops it from opening. At which moment we hear voices
    outside.)*

HAZARD. Hurry up!
BLACK DOG.
He's inside!
DEATH.

It's time to kill him!

BLIND PEW.

Hands, head around to the back o' the house
So they can't get away!

HAZARD.

Aye aye, sir.

*(JIM and his mother look at each other with horror – and start
piling tables and chairs in front of the door.)*

BLIND PEW.

Now open the door.

(The Pirates try the door.)

DEATH.

It's locked!

BLIND PEW.

Break it down!

BLACK DOG.

Set to it lads!

DEATH.

Put your shoulders into it!

*(Bang! Bang! JIM looks desperately around the room – then
takes his mother's arm and sweeps them both behind the
curtains. The door bursts open and the PIRATES tumble in
– BLACK DOG, GEORGE MERRY, JUSTICE DEATH and
BLIND PEW. Simultaneously, EZEKIEL HAZARD hurries
in from the back. PEW is crazed with anger.)*

BLACK DOG.
There's Bones!
    MERRY.
              And there's his chest!
    HAZARD.
                      Bones!
Bones, wake up!
    DEATH.
              He's dead.
    BLACK DOG.
                    Dead?
    BLIND PEW.
                    Dead?!
(Kicking the corpse.)
Damn your eyes, you stinkin' pirate! I was
Lookin' forward to killin' ya meself!
Now empty the chest and bring me the map and make it quick!

(The PIRATES empty the chest onto the floor.)

BLACK DOG.
I don't see it!
    DEATH.
              It ain't here no place!
    HAZARD.
Look at the linin'. It's been ripped open.
Somebody's took out the map already.
    DEATH.
Who?
    MERRY.
              Who?!

BLACK DOG.

Who?!

DEATH.

Who was it?!

BLIND PEW.

…That little pup. It's him. I'll rip his head off.
I'll pull his fingers from his hands! I'll squeeze
His neck until the pus runs out of his eyes.
Where is he?!
*(At which moment, out of fear, MOTHER makes a noise, shifting
the curtains slightly.)*
What was that?

BLACK DOG.

What?

BLIND PEW.

I heard somethin'.

MERRY.

It was upstairs.

DEATH.

Right above us.

BLACK DOG.

Come on!

HAZARD.

Let's get him!

BLACK DOG.

Hurry up!

DEATH.

Pew, shake a leg!!

*(As the PIRATES clatter up the stairs, JIM and his MOTHER
come out of hiding. Then they see that PEW is still in the*

middle of the room, waiting for a sound. JIM and his
mother freeze; then they tiptoe towards the door, but PEW
hears them and cries out. Using his stick, he tries to touch
them – and he almost does. But they evade his stick and
continue to tiptoe toward the door. Finally, they get away.
At that moment, the other PIRATES hurry down the stairs.)

BLIND PEW.
Hands! Justice! The boy's nearby, I just heard him!
Scatter the men and squeeze the bloody hills!
Look under every bush and rock and...God 'amighty!
If I had a pair of eyes, I'd find him meself
And tear his eyeballs out!

(The action shifts to the front of the inn – as JIM and his
MOTHER run for their lives. As they run, JIM'S MOTHER
stumbles, twisting her ankle.)

JIM.
Hurry, Mother!
MOTHER.
I can't walk...You go, Jim...
   JIM. You have to, Mother! Don't you see, they're pirates!
They'll kill us!
   MOTHER. But I can't move!
   JIM. Yes you can. Just hold my arm. Quick! Over here,
under the pilings!

(As they hide themselves behind the pilings, PEW hurtles out
of the door, followed by the other PIRATES. Before the
men can start their search, we hear a loud whistle in the

distance: *"Oweeee!" The PIRATES stop cold.)*

DEATH.
Wait! What's that?!
HAZARD.
                    Shhh!
MERRY.
                              The signal from Dirk.
It's trouble, gentlemen.

*(We hear the sound of galloping horses and two shots in the
    distance.)*

DEATH.
                It's the militia!
HAZARD.
Let's budge, and quick! We'll meet back at the ship!
BLIND PEW.
(Outraged)
"Budge," you skulk?! It's no time to budge!
You've got to scatter and find that stinkin' boy!
He's got the map!
MERRY.
It's no use squallin', Pew. Now shake a leg.

*(The PIRATES scatter and disappear, leaving PEW alone. He's
    outraged.)*

BLIND PEW.
Hey! Ya cowards! Ya no-good tunbelly swabs!
Ezekiel Hazard! Justice Death! Anne Bonny!

You should all be wasted yerselves for turnin' yellow!
(He swings his sword, trying to hit them.)
There! That'll teach ya! And *there!* And *there!*
(The horses are getting louder and louder.)
Boys ...? Boys, don't leave me! You can't leave
A poor blind beggar man out here in this
Black and shiverin' wasteland...
Help! Please help! They're comin'!
Ahhhhhhhhhhhhhhhhhhhhhhhhh!!

(He gets run down by a team of horses and the coach behind it.
It's a gruesome and magnificent death. Then, DR. LIVESY
rushes in, followed by SQUIRE TRELAWNEY, an open-
faced, middle-aged man of ample means.)

DR. LIVESY. Jim?! *Jim Hawkins?!* Squire, look inside.
Please.
TRELAWNEY. Right you are!

(As TRELAWNEY disappears into the inn, JIM and his MOTHER
rush out of hiding.)

JIM. Dr. Livesy! Mother, come on. It'll be all right now.
DR. LIVESY. Jim. Mrs. Hawkins. Thank God. Have you
been hurt?
MRS. HAWKINS. We're fine –
JIM. But they were *pirates*, sir! *Real pirates!* They were
after Mr. Bones. One of them was called Black Dog, and he
and Mr. Bones had a fight! And there was another one who was
called...*(He sees the remains of PEW.)* That's him. He wanted
to kill me.

DR. LIVESY. Well then good riddance to him.

(SQUIRE TRELAWNEY comes out of the inn.)

TRELAWNEY. *(Jolly)* All safe inside. Place is a bit of a mess, though. All rumpsy-dervy. Rugs up. Spoons. Plate. Gad, if I'd ha' crossed swords with the beggars! Made mincemeat of 'em! Fighting man, by nature. Trained as a lad. Sword. Pike. Oh, and there's a dead man inside.
DR. LIVESY. Dead?
TRELAWNEY. Mm. On the floor. Like a slab of beef.
MRS. HAWKINS. Oh, dear ...

(She hurries into the inn.)

TRELAWNEY. Ma'am, I wouldn't go in there if I was... *(She's gone.)* Domestic instincts. Admirable. Three cheers.
DR. LIVESY. Squire, this is Jim Hawkins. The lad I told you about. Jim, Squire Trelawney.
JIM. How do you do, sir.
TRELAWNEY. Pleasure, lad. Brave boy.
DR. LIVESY. Jim, I wonder what they were after. Why tear the place apart after Bones was dead?
JIM. I think I know, sir, I...

(He stops himself.)

DR. LIVESY. You can talk in front of Squire Trelawney. He's one of my oldest friends.
JIM. Well, sir. I think it was this.
TRELAWNEY. A map!

DR. LIVESY. It appears to be an island. But where?

TRELAWNEY. "Bearings: Longitude, 62 degrees 17' 20" West. Latitude 10 degrees, 2'40" North.

DR. LIVESY. Look, there's writing at the bottom.

TRELAWNEY. "Instructions."

DR. LIVESY. "Currents."

TRELAWNEY. "Danger: Skeleton Island!"

JIM. And look, sir! Do you see them? Three little crosses in red ink. And this one has writing next to it. I can't quite make it out...

TRELAWNEY. Let's see, let's see! "Bulk of treasure here." Signed "J. Flint, Captain." *(Overcome, he sits.)* Oh my Lord ...

DR. LIVESY. "Captain Flint"?

JIM. Have you heard of him, sir?

TRELAWNEY. Heard of him?! Bloodthirstiest buccaneer that ever trawled a deck! Blackbeard? – a child to Flint!

DR. LIVESY. But would the treasure amount to much? That's the question.

TRELAWNEY. "Amount"? sir? "Amount"? Hee, hee, ha, ha!

(Singing, dancing a jig.)

"THERE WAS A YOUNG LAD ON THE SEA, THE SEA
THERE WAS A YOUNG LAD ON THE SEAAAAA!"

I'll tell you amount. There isn't a sailor alive who hasn't heard the stories. Pearls the size of ostrich eggs; rubies, red as blood, of such rarity you can't look at 'em more than a minute without burning your eyeballs. Jade from the dark green East so fine that you can see your own reflection in it. And gold...more gold than a pasha has, or a king or emperor! "Amount"? It amounts to the following: with this map in our possession – with this clue, this oyster of information – I will fit out a ship in Bristol dock – assemble a crew entire – lay the provisions – hire a captain – all at my own expense. And I'll take you, Livesy, as the ship's doctor, and Hawkins here as cabin boy, and I'll have that treasure for the three of us if I search a year! Two years! Five years! I will not rest until it's in the hold. Are you with me, lads?

JIM. Will it be dangerous, sir?

TRELAWNEY. Dangerous?   D'ya think it's a country dance to go to Bristol, then across the waters, through the jungle, up a hill and clunk, I think I'll take this pirate treasure *can I have another LEMONADE!!! Of course it's dangerous!* Now is it yes or no? Right now. Are you with me? Doctor?

DR. LIVESY. … Yes.

TRELAWNEY. Hawkins?

JIM. Aye, aye, sir!

TRELAWNEY. Ha, ha! That's the lad!

(Singing and dancing.)

"AND HE DREAMED OF HIS LASSIE, HE DREAMED OF
     HIS HOME,

BUT MOSTLY HE DREAMED OF THE SEA, THE SEA,

MOSTLY HE DREAMED OF THE SEA! HEY!"

*(As TRELAWNEY sings and jigs, JIM turns to us, overlapping
     the song, which fades away:)*

JIM. And so our fates were sealed. We were after treasure and there was no turning back. *(As JIM continues, THE SET CHANGES. The inn fades away and is replaced by the dock at Bristol, which grows before us.)* That week, Dr. Livesy went to London to find a physician to take his practice, while Squire

Trelawney went to Bristol to find his treasure ship. He swore he didn't call it that in public; but Dr. Livesy said – only half-jokingly, I think – that the only man he feared in this enterprise was the squire himself, because he couldn't hold his tongue.

TRELAWNEY.

"... the sea, the sea,

There was a young lad on the seaaaaaaa!"

JIM. I shared Dr. Livesy's concern. It seemed a lifetime, but it was a bare four weeks before the squire wrote to say that he had acquired a ship: a schooner called The Hispaniola.

TRELAWNEY.

"And a finer, sleeker friend of a sailor you'll never meet in all England, laddie!"

JIM. I said my fond farewells to my mother, then traveled overnight by coach and arrived in Bristol just as the sun was rising in the East. "But look, the morn in russet mantle clad Walks o'er the dew of yon high eastward hill." My father's ghost was not far away that morning, speaking *Hamlet* in my ear; and his presence gave me both comfort and longing.

Scene 3

(We're now on the dock in Bristol in the early morning. The place is teeming with exotic life. In the distance, we see great ships of all sizes, rigs and nations, bobbing on the water. Along the dock, we see sailors singing at their work; admirals with polished boots; ladies strolling with parasols for the sun; oystermen with rings in their ears; and seamen ranged high aloft, hanging to threads that seem no thicker than a spider's web.

After a moment, LONG JOHN SILVER ENTERS. We will come to know him for his strength, his courage, his quickness

and his magnificent geniality. He has only one leg, uses a crutch and is carrying a bird cage with a parrot inside.
A moment later, JIM ENTERS, dazzled by his new surroundings and is approached by a tattered BEGGAR.)

BEGGAR. Good morning, matey. You're lookin' as trim as a jibsail you are.

JIM. Thank you very much.

BEGGAR. Got a few spare pennies for a poor lost sailor?

JIM. I-I'm sorry, I don't.

BEGGAR. What about that purse, eh? It looks right heavy it does and full o' gold and silver, eh?

JIM. No, I'm afraid there's not much inside – *(The beggar cuts JIM'S purse, grabs it and starts to run.)* Hey! Stop! Help! Someone! He stole my purse! Stop him!

(As the BEGGAR runs past, SILVER uses his crutch and sends the man flying. The BEGGAR ends up flat on his back with SILVER'S crutch on his chest, pinning him to the ground.)

BEGGAR. *Ahh!*
SILVER.
Well, well. Look'ee what the brine
And bubblin' sea has coughed up.

BEGGAR. Silver!
SILVER.
Takin' somethin' of a shortcut, are we Mr. Blakely?

BEGGAR. Ow!
SILVER.
And what be that you're clutchin' to your chest
Like the baby Jesus?

BEGGAR. Get orff! Get orff me! Taint none o' your

business!

*(The BEGGAR tries to get away, but SILVER uses his crutch to
    subdue him.)*

>   **BEGGAR.** *Ow! Ow! Ow!*
>   **SILVER.**

What shall we do with him, lad? Eh?
Feed him to the empty sharks, or hand him
Over to the law and let them stretch his neck?

>   **JIM.** I'd hate to see him hang, sir.
>   **SILVER.**

Right. Sharks it is.

(SILVER drags the BEGGAR to the edge of the dock.)

>   **BEGGAR.**

No! No! No! Please! I can't swim!

>   **SILVER.**

Ohhh ... get out. Out! *Out!*
Just make certain I never see your snivelin'
Face again, cause if I do the sharks
Will have a dainty little breakfast treat,
And believe me they won't mind the gristle.
(He releases the BEGGAR, who starts to leave.)
Eh, eh, eh.

*(He motions to the BEGGAR to return JIM'S purse – which he
    does reluctantly.)*

>   **BEGGAR.** I'll get ya for this!

SILVER.
Then do it quick, cause I'm gettin' bored with life.

(And the BEGGAR'S gone.)

JIM. Thank you, sir.
SILVER. Don't mention it, lad. Just be more careful with
that purse o' yours. *(The parrot speaks up: "Pieces of eight!*
Pieces of eight!")
Aw, look at him, he's gettin' hungry.
I should a' fed him that squirmin' devil there –
Though on second thought, it might have poisoned
The poor bird. Ha ha ha ha ha ha ha!

(This strikes SILVER as truly funny and he laughs so heartily
that JIM can't help joining in.)

JIM. Is he a real parrot?
SILVER.
Well, he is and he ain't, ya might say.
I brought him back meself from Madagascar,
But I suspect he's partly Toucan.
JIM. I'll bet he's a very good companion, sir. If you're
ever lonely.
SILVER.
That he is, lad. A fine friend when a
Friend is needed. We sail together, like Juno's swans.
(JIM starts at the quotation.)
And why be you here, on this dock in Bristol?
Run away from home to taste the sea?
JIM. No, sir. Well, in a way, but not exactly. I mean, my

mother knows all about it.

SILVER.

Ah.

JIM.

I'm to be cabin boy on a ship that sails in a few days. The Hispaniola. I hope to acquit myself with dignity.

SILVER.

Well that's the lad! Good for you, boy!

And somethin' tells me you'll do it, too.

You're smart as paint you are.

I saw that when I first set eyes on you.

I was a cabin boy meself once –

On a cutter it was in the Indian Sea.

And up I rose like the phoenix from the fire

To the glorious title of ship's cook, thence to

Quartermaster and then midshipman on a

Man-o'-war – oh, I was a devil with a double quadrant –

And I'd ha' made leftenant too if I hadn't

Lost me leg in the service o' the King.

Under Admiral Hawke it was –

Finest sailor that ever cruised the sea.

JIM. Are you sailing with any of these ships here?

SILVER.

Ah, don't I wish it, lad. But nobody wants a

Sea cook with a game leg.

THE BIRD. Pieces of eight! Pieces of eight!

SILVER. Me friend here's gettin' hungry. I'd best go feed him. *(Puts out his hand.)* John Silver.

JIM. Jim Hawkins.

SILVER.

"Hawkins"? I knew a Hawkins once, but far from here, in

Londontown. Got relatives?

JIM. No sir. I mean not in London. But my father went there once.

SILVER.

A different Hawkins, I'll wager.

(He heads off.)

        This was some years back.

(He's almost gone.)

                His name was Peter.

JIM. ... My father's name was Peter.

SILVER. Peter Hawkins. He spoke of a son in Dorset. At a place called ... Black Hill Cove, I think.

JIM. *(Almost dumb with excitement.)*...You knew my father. That was him! That was his last trip! He went to London for his health!

SILVER.

That's right! He came for the sawbones!

Well I'll be...Peter Hawkins. We was

Mates, Jim! The very best o' friends!

JIM. I can't believe it!

SILVER.

Here, let me look at you ...

Why there is a resemblance! A strong one.

He was a good cook, as I remember. Ran a tavern like.

JIM. Yes!

SILVER.

He was always quotin' his Shakespeare, he was.

Fair crammed it down me own throat as well.

"O for a muse o' fire that would ascend

The brightest heaven of invention."

JIM.

"A kingdom for a stage, princes to act

And monarchs to behold the swelling scene!"

Ha ha!

SILVER.

Ha ha ha ha ha!

Wait a moment. Look at this. I've got it right here …

(He pats his pockets and finds a small, tattered copy of the plays.)

This was his. He gave it to me afore he died.

JIM. *(In awe.)* His Shakespeare. It's his. Look, it has his writing in it!

SILVER.

I got to confess, he asked me special to hand it

To ya if I ever found meself in Devon.

But after that I went to sea and…anyway.

Here. It's yours.

JIM. Mine…

SILVER. I ask yer pardon, Jim. I should a' found you before this.

JIM. No! No…I'm just so glad that …

(He's overcome with emotion and turns away.)

SILVER. You're a good boy, Jim. Your dad would be proud of you.

(At this moment, SQUIRE TRELAWNEY appears.)

TRELAWNEY. Jim Hawkins. Bless my soul. Right on time, boy. Punctual. Top notch.

JIM. Good morning, sir.

TRELAWNEY. Is something wrong? Are you…?

JIM. No, sir, I'm fine. How-how's the ship? Is she in harbor?

TRELAWNEY. In harbor? Boy, you're almost standing next to her. There. Look. Two red flags. The Hispaniola.

SILVER. Oh, ain't she a pretty thing. Looks handy as a dolphin and twice as quick.

TRELAWNEY. That she is, sir. Sails like the wind.

SILVER. Is she ketch-rigged?

TRELAWNEY. Right to the yardarm. Like a lace handkerchief. Carries 200 tons. Do I know you, sir?

SILVER. John Silver, at your pleasure.

JIM. He was a friend of my father's! This is Squire Trelawney. It's his ship.

SILVER. Pleased to make your acquaintance, sir. And I'll tell ya this: you've got yourself the finest cabin boy I ever set me eyes on. Smart as paint, he is. And good as gold.

JIM. He stopped a villain from stealing my purse just now! You should have seen him! Knocked him down! He's as strong as Hercules!

SILVER. Oh now Jim, let's not exaggerate. He'd a' fallen over with a puff o' wind.

JIM. He might have saved my life! Who knows what the villain would have done!

SILVER. Now, now.

JIM. Sir, do you think…do you think Mr. Silver could sail with us?

SILVER. Now Jim just stop it! What would the squire here want with an old sea cook with a game leg.

JIM. He sailed with Admiral Hawke!

TRELAWNEY. Really? Well. Hawke was the best.

SILVER. Finest sailor ever lived, he was. Taught me everything.

TRELAWNEY. And you're a cook?

SILVER.

Cook, midshipman, quartermaster.

If it be on water, I tend to con

The why and wherefore.

TRELAWNEY. And you're looking for a berth?

SILVER. That I am. But I ain't one to push meself.

TRELAWNEY. Well Hawkins here thinks a lot of you. And our trouble is, we don't have much of a crew yet. I've hired a captain – fellow named Smollett. Do you know him?

SILVER. No sir.

TRELAWNEY. He's trying to get a crew together but says all the sailors in Bristol are engaged.

SILVER. Maybe he's askin' the wrong people.

TRELAWNEY. Meaning?

SILVER. Meanin' you gotta shoot high enough to bring down the prize. You'll be wantin' a crackerjack crew with a ship like that. The best in Bristol. And I knows every one of 'em. I've sailed with 'em all. On the Swallow and the Caravan, from Malabar to the Barbary Coast. And believe me, they'll make 'emselves available for a good voyage. Where do you sail?

TRELAWNEY. Ah. Secret. Can't tell. But between you and me...there's a *treasure* involved.

JIM. Sir!

SILVER. A treasure?

TRELAWNEY. Enormous! Magnificent! The greatest of the century! And it's not in doubt, sir, I assure you. It's Flint's treasure. Captain Flint.

SILVER. The pirate?

TRELAWNEY. That's him. And the word is – all over – not just me – ask anyone, sir – it's a king's ransom in jewels and gold! And we'll have it! Without question!

SILVER. Sir...if you let me – and you've got to give me your proxy like so I can make the bargains – I will get you the finest crew that ever sailed from Bristol Harbor. I'll stake me life on it.

TRELAWNEY. You really think you can do it?
SILVER.

In a flash of lightnin'.

"And ere a man hath power to say 'Behold',"

JIM.

"The jaws of darkness do devour it up."

BOTH.

"So quick bright things come to confusion."

(They both smile and TRELAWNEY is bewildered.)

SILVER. Well?

TRELAWNEY. ...... Done, sir. *(JIM whoops happily.)* I like the cut of your jib, Mr. Silver. We have a deal.

SILVER. And here's me hand.

JIM. Sir! Sir! When do we start?!

TRELAWNEY. At this point, that depends on Silver.

SILVER. I'll have your crew in three days' time, and that's a promise.

TRELAWNEY. In which case, we sail by the end of the week! Ha ha! *(JIM whoops again.)* Oh just wait'll I tell Livesy. I'll go find him. Boy, I'll meet you here at three o'clock and we'll inspect the ship together. Silver – get to work. Well done, boy! Good lad! Ha ha!

(He's gone.)

(Music begins to play.)

    SILVER. You brought me luck, Jim. And we have your father to thank for it.

    JIM. We do, don't we.

(Suddenly, JIM embraces SILVER, who holds the boy for a moment.)

    SILVER.
Come along. I got work to do.
And you've got a feathered friend o' mine to take care of.
(The bird.)
His name, by the way, is Captain Flint.
Just like the pirate.

(They EXIT together in the fading light.)

Scene 4

(The Hispaniola. We hear a sailor's cry – then another – as the Hispaniola takes shape in front of us.)

    THE CREW.
Barrels o' water, comin' through!
Stow 'em below!
Aye, aye, sir!
Hold fast to the mainsheet, for the love o' God!

And pipe the orders!

("Oweeeeeeeeeeeeeeeeeeeeeeeeeeee!" As the pipe sounds its loud, shrill note, JIM appears and addresses the audience. By this time, we've noticed that the crew is made up of Pirates, including ISRAEL HANDS, ANNE BONNY, JOSIAH BLAND, JUSTICE DEATH and GEORGE MERRY.)

JIM. As he promised, Mr. Silver delivered a crew by the end of the week. Our only delays after that were occasioned by the arguments between Squire Trelawney and Mr. Smollett, the captain he had hired some weeks before. They were oil and water and argued about *everything.*

(SMOLLETT, TRELAWNEY and DR. LIVESY cross the stage.)

TRELAWNEY. And the problem *this time,* sir?!

SMOLLETT. There is no "this time" about it, sir. It is the same problem I have broached before.

DR. LIVESY. Which is?

SMOLLETT. I don't like this cruise and I don't like the men!

TRELAWNEY. Well perhaps you don't like the *ship,* sir!

SMOLLETT. She seems a clever craft – *but I haven't sailed her yet, have I?!*

DR. LIVESY. You say you don't like the cruise, sir. Why is that?

SMOLLETT. I was engaged on what we call sealed orders to sail *this* ship for *that* gentleman when and where he should bid me. So far so good. But now I find that every man before the mast knows more than I do.

TRELAWNEY. Such as?

SMOLLETT. Such as that we're looking for treasure! And as for the men, I should have had the choosing of them. I'm the captain.

TRELAWNEY. You had the choosing, but you couldn't find them!

SMOLLETT. You don't find a good crew overnight!

TRELAWNEY. Well Silver did, now didn't he?!

SMOLLETT. Not in my opinion, no he didn't!

DR. LIVESY. Gentlemen, please! What is it you wish at this juncture, Captain?

SMOLLETT.

First point: The crew is now loading the powder and arms in the fore-hold – but you have a good place under *our* cabins, so put them there where we can keep an eye on them. Second point: Squire, you have two of your own men with you, as well as the boy Hawkins. Give them berths right here, beside our cabins. Then all our allies are together.

DR. LIVESY. In other words, you fear a mutiny.

SMOLLETT. I didn't say that. But I ask you to take certain precautions or let me resign.

TRELAWNEY. … Fine, *fine!* Do as you please! Move the powder and the men, but know this: I am extremely irked. Good day, sir!

(As the men walk out, DR. LIVESY gives JIM a look of exasperation.)

JIM. *(To the audience.)* And so the time came at last for our voyage to begin. *(Church bells sound.)* On Sunday morning we went to church where the Squire, Dr. Livesy, Mr. Silver and I asked for a special blessing for our journey – for safety, good health and blessed peace. *(All four kneel for a moment in the* *light of a church.)* That night came the final bustle as everything was stowed in place. *(Sailors appear and go about their work.)* Then, a little before dawn, the boatswain sounded his pipe *("Oweeeee!")* and as the sky turned red with the first beams of morning, we headed out into the open sea, as the Hispaniola began her voyage to the Isle of Treasure.

(Grand music sounds.

During JIM'S speech above, as the sailors turn the heavy capstan that pulls the anchor out of the water, the whole ship comes to life for the first time. The deck, the masts, the rigging, everything gleams with an exotic air of romance and adventure. The sky is red and streaked with golden sunlight, and we see the vast horizon in the distance, beckoning us on to lands unknown.)

THE CREW.
Ship o' the line, fore and aft!
Report from the crow's nest!
Clean ahead and hold her steady!

(The ship sails serenely on the water. A moment of calm. The lights and music change to denote the passing of time. It is now days later. We see LONG JOHN SILVER sitting on deck, peeling potatoes. After a moment, JIM walks by.)

SILVER. Jim Hawins, lad! – and how be you this bright glorious mornin'?
JIM. Well, thank you.
SILVER.
Come and have a yarn with old John.

Nobody be more welcome than yourself, Jim.
"Small cheer and great welcome make a merry feast."
> **JIM.** Can I help?
> **SILVER.**

You may indeed. I reckon you know how to peel a potato?
> **JIM.** I think so.

(JIM tries one – taking away more potato than he does skin.)

> **SILVER.**

Try and get just the skin if you can. Like this. *(JIM watches SILVER, then tries again.)* There. Much better.

(They peel for a moment, side by side.)

> **JIM.** I'm-I'm sorry you have to do work like this. I'll wager that on your other ships you had assistants and-and scullions and things.
> **SILVER.**

"Sorry?!" For peelin' potatoes?! Jim-lad, don't you
Never be sorry for doin' an honest day's work,
No matter what the task. Why, just think of all
The good we're doin' right this minute.
First of all, we're givin' our arms and fingers
A bit o' exercise, makin' 'em strong as steel,
All the better to do our other jobs
In life when the time comes along.
Second, we create a thing of beauty
With this here potato, like the good Lord done himself
On the Day o' Creation by compounding the likes
Of you and me. Just look at this masterpiece,

Ready to jump into a pot o' boilin'
Water out o' sheer vanity. Ha!
Why I've seen gals on tobacco papers who ain't
As pretty as that. O' course I never put
Me lips on 'em the way I does a potato,
And that might change me point o' view.
Third, we get our mouths a-waterin' just by
Smellin' this here perfume, which means
We're sure to do the good Lord's work at suppertime
And clean our plates like our mothers taught us,
God bless their souls. Fourth, we're keepin'
The crew what eats these potatoes strong and healthy
So they can bring us all home safe and sound.
Five, we're drawin' blood from our fingers now and then
So's we never has to play the piano;
Six, we're keepin' ourselves out o' trouble;
And seven, we're stealin' a few extra minutes
To enjoy each other's company, and there ain't
Nothin' to compare to that on the seven seas
Now is there? So you tell me what's better
Than peelin' a potato. Eh?

("Oweeeee!" ISRAEL HANDS appears from below.)

HANDS. Hey Silver, you're wanted below decks – by the captain.
SILVER. Do you know what he's after?
HANDS. Not a clue. But I think it's all right.

(They exchange a look, which JIM notices.)

SILVER. I'll be right back, Jim. And don't you do all o' them potatoes before I'm returned.

(LONG JOHN EXITS into the hold, leaving JIM and HANDS alone.)

JIM. Have you known Mr. Silver for very long?

HANDS. What, Barbecue? Long ain't the word. We been from Surinam to the Spanish Main together. I knows him like the back o' me hand. He's brave as a lion. I saw him lose his leg, from a cannon shot off the coast o' Tripoli. Mangled it were. Then they ampytates it durin' the battle, right on deck, and he just watches 'em do it and don't utter a sound. Puh. *Now* look at 'im – peelin' potatas.

JIM. He seems happy with the voyage.

HANDS. Well o' course he's happy! He's lookin' forward to gettin' the –

(He stops himself.)

JIM. Getting what?

HANDS. … Nothin'. Gettin' to the island, that's all. *(He laughs uncomfortably; then his eyes narrow. He has an idea.)* Tell me somethin'. Now you knows that I's always liked ya. Jest the way old John does. I think o' you like a mate. Ya see? Israel Hands and Jim…

JIM. Hawkins.

HANDS. Hawkins. Right. So give it to me, straight, all right? Is it you that gots the map?

JIM. Map?

HANDS. The map o' the island, what shows the treasure.

JIM. I-I don't know what you're talking about.

HANDS. O' course you do. Does ya keep it on ya? In yer jacket?

(HANDS starts backing JIM against the rail, becoming more and more threatening.)

JIM. I-I don't know what you mean …

HANDS. I ain't had much in me life, I can tell ya that. Ain't had no schoolin', see – but I can memorize a map in seconds, which might do us a power o' good –

JIM. Please – !

HANDS. I jest want a gander at it to fill me eyes!

JIM. Stop it!

HANDS. I want to touch it between me fingers so's I can start a-dreamin' and makin' plans – !

(He grabs JIM roughly, about to injure him.)

JIM. *Stop!*
HANDS. *Now give it over! I jest want to feel it!*
JIM. *Get away!*

(They struggle for a moment – when CAPT. SMOLLETT ENTERS.)

SMOLLETT.
Mr. Hands!
JIM. Captain Smollett!

(HANDS backs away.)

SMOLLETT. Is there a problem?!

HANDS. No, *sir*.

SMOLLETT. I'm glad to hear it. Now go to your duties.
Now! (HANDS EXITS.) You too, Hawkins.

JIM. Yes, sir.

SMOLLETT. And stay out of trouble.

JIM. I'll try, sir.

(SMOLLETT EXITS. JIM turns to the audience:)

JIM. The next day, I tried to tell John what happened with
Mr. Hands, but he said I must have misunderstood. I knew he
was wrong, but I had no suspicion then that my encounter with
Hands was merely the beginning of a longer nightmare that
would come to a treacherous and bloody end.

*(The moon rises and the deck of the ship becomes deeply
      shadowed. During the following, JIM climbs into an apple
      barrel and, although we can see him, he's hidden from the
      view of those onstage.)*

JIM. It began with a barrel of apples which stood broached
in the waist of the ship for anyone to help himself. It was just
after sundown in the third week of our voyage, and it occurred
to me that I should like an apple before turning in. The barrel
was so huge that I had to climb inside, where I found scarce
any apples left; but sitting down there in the dark, what with the
sound of the water and the rocking movement of the ship, I had
either fallen asleep or was on the point of doing so when a noise
jostled me to my senses.

(The PIRATES ENTER, having a private meeting. They include SILVER, HANDS, ANNE BONNY, JUSTICE DEATH, JOSIAH BLAND and GEORGE MERRY. And JIM squints out through an opening between two slats of the barrel; thus he manages to watch as well as hear the following.)

HANDS. *I* says we do it *now*, John, when they ain't suspectin'.

SILVER. Israel –

HANDS. We could overpower 'em in a minute – then kill 'em all! But I wants the cap'n for meself. I'm gonna wring 'is little calf's head off his body.

SILVER. You can wring it all ya like, but we ain't ready yet.

MERRY. And I says why not.

SILVER. Because, you jellied eel, we ain't got the map!

BONNY. We believe it's on the boy.

SILVER.

And what if it ain't? What if Smollett has it,

Or the doctor? Or maybe they've hidden it away

Someplace. Hanh? *Then* how do we find the island?

MERRY. We grab the boy and swear that we'll kill him if they don't hand us the map. Or just massacre 'em and find it ourselves. We have the muskets put away.

PIRATES.

I agree./Let's just get on with it. /That's the plan.

SILVER.

Would ya listen to me, ya dumb pirates! Gad!

There ain't the brains of a dyin' oyster among ya!

Why take that kind o' risk? Hanh?

Jest bide yer time.

With the likes o' you it's always hurry it up,
Do it now and the bleedin' devil take it –
Which is why, when all is over and done with,
I'll be ridin' to Parlyment in a Crystal
Carriage, and all o' you 'ull be chained up
In Execution Dock waitin' to be hanged!
Now here's what I say and ya better listen:
We don't make a move till we've been to the island
And all the gold's on board.

    MERRY. And I says that's too long to wait.

    SILVER.

And *I* says who's in charge o' this operation
And was chose by all o' ya?!

    MERRY. And I says that's a mighty nice question and maybe we ought to choose again. Maybe you're getting soft with that one leg missing – and maybe you ain't the man you was and somebody named George Merry ought to be in charge!

(SILVER glares at MERRY and is about to attack him, but HANDS restrains him with a touch of the arm.)

    BLAND. John. Assumin' we wait till the gold's on board, *then* what'll we do with the lubbers?

    SILVER. Ah. Now you're thinkin'. That's a business inquiry, that is. And we got two choices. We could leave 'em there on the island like maroons – that was Blackbeard's way – or cut 'em down like that much pork, like Flint would a' done.

    PIRATES. Cut 'em down, says I! / And I! / And wring their necks!

    BONNY. *Pssssst!* Hold on! There's Tom comin'.

(TOM MORGAN ENTERS. He's a young sailor and clearly nervous.)

DEATH. Is he with us? Did you ask him?

BONNY. I did and he ain't decided yet.

HANDS. Tom, over here!

PIRATES. Hello, Tom./There he is./And welcome.

SILVER. Well how's old Tom, eh?

TOM. I'm all right.

HANDS. We're havin' a meetin'.

BONNY. About you know what.

TOM. That's what I thought.

SILVER.

Now at the moment we's talkin' about money. Right, boys?

("Uh huh./Money./That's right.")

Which might just interest ya, who knows. Eh?

(They all laugh.)

Ya see, Gentlemen o' Fortune, like ourselves,

We *make* money, and a lot of it.

We live rough and we risk swingin',

But when the cruise is done, it's hundreds o' pounds

A-linin' our pockets. And then we eat like

Potentates and drink like the laughin' gods.

We live in mansions like the Duke o' Buckingham

And have adventures like the Three Musketeers.

And women? Hah! They fawn upon us in little

Skimpy costumes, poppin' grapes into our mouths,

And figs dipped in buttered rum and sugar.

Back home I have me own barber

What shaves me every day and clips me hair,
Me own cook who makes me partridges in
Berry sauce, me own tailor for me duds,
And a man I pay who's old and blind to sit and
Tell me the Arabian Nights and lull me
To sleep on me satin pillow.
Now o' course you're young and ain't had much experience –
But you're smart as paint you are.
I see that when I first set eyes on you.

*(We see JIM flinch at this. These are the very words that SILVER
used with JIM, and he feels betrayed.)*

   SILVER.
And so I'm talkin' to you like a man,
And I'm waitin' for a man's answer.
Are ya with us, laddie, or not? Yes or no.
And bear in mind we ain't decided yet
To do a thing to even raise an eyebrow,
And this'll likely be a nice peaceful voyage,
Right up till we get back home again
And return to resting in our own soft beds.
   TOM. R-right. Well. Here's where I stand. I-I've given
it a lot of thought and...I think I'd rather...for now at least...
remain where I am, with the Squire and the Captain and Dr.
Livesy. I'm just not sure I'm meant to be a...
   SILVER. Gentleman of Fortune?
   TOM. Right. Yes. For now at least. So...that's how things
stand.
   SILVER. Understood. I can respect that. And so can
we all. *(The others murmur assent, though they're not very*

convincing. SILVER stands up and shakes TOM'S hand.) And
so I'll wish ya good night and God speed.

    TOM. Thank you.

*(As TOM turns to go, SILVER and HANDS exchange a look.
TOM gets part way across the deck when SILVER whips
his crutch out of his armpit and hurls it into TOM'S back
with stunning violence. TOM lets out a horrible cry and
falls to the ground.)*

    TOM. *Ahhhhhhhh!*

*(The other PIRATES run to the body and examine it. Meanwhile,
we see that JIM is horrified beyond words.)*

    DEATH. He's dead.
    MERRY. His back's broken.

*(The PIRATES are in awe of SILVER. Even GEORGE MERRY
is impressed.)*

    SILVER.
Throw him overboard. We'll say he must have
Fallen over the rail by accident.

*(As the PIRATES pick TOM up and heave him overboard, they
see something in the moonlight.)*

    PIRATES.
Wait!
Look!

The island!
There it is in the moonlight!
Call the captain!
    SILVER.
No! Let the lookout on the crow's nest spot it.
And get to yer bunks! Quick double time!
If they see us all grouped up like a mess o' clams
They'll turn suspicious. Now get a-movin'!

*(The PIRATES scatter. SILVER is almost gone when he
    remembers something.)*

Apple.

*(He hobbles over to the barrel and is about to put his hand
    inside, when the sailor in the crow's nest cries:)*

    SAILOR.
(Off)
Land ho!

*(SILVER shakes his head in disappointment and hurries off. The
    moment SILVER is gone, JIM emerges from the barrel.)*

    JIM. *(To the audience.)* As you can imagine, I felt the
keenness of this serpent's betrayal to the deepest soundings of
my immortal soul. For a moment, I could barely stir a finger;
then, suddenly there was a great rush of feet across the deck. I
could hear sailors tumbling up from the cabin and the foc's'le;
and slipping instantly outside my barrel, I dived behind the
foresail, made a double towards the stern, then gathered our

allies in the captain's cabin where I told them everything.

(We're now at one side of the ship, in the captain's cabin, where SMOLLETT, TRELAWNEY, LIVESY and JIM are gathered.)

SMOLLETT.
I knew it!
TRELAWNEY.
The scoundrel!
DR. LIVESY. The remarkable thing is that Silver has kept it so quiet.

SMOLLETT. Because Silver is a very remarkable man.

TRELAWNEY. He'd look remarkably well hanging from a yardarm!

JIM. *(Exploding)* I *trusted* him! He was so *kind!* And he knew my ...!

SMOLLETT. The question now is what do we do.

(The action shifts to the other end of the ship, where we see GEORGE MERRY, JUSTICE DEATH and ANNE BONNY. Seeing the two camps at opposite ends of the stage, each in its own theatrical space, should remind us of a Shakespearean history play.)

MERRY. *I tell you, boys, it's now or never!* We've gained the island and it's time to strike!

BONNY. But Silver said –

MERRY. *Who cares what Silver said?!* Use your nut! Right now we have the advantage because they don't suspect us.

DEATH. But what about the map?

MERRY. We grab the boy and threaten to kill him.

BONNY. What if they say go ahead?

MERRY. *That ain't gonna happen! They ain't ruthless, selfish killers! They're not like us!!* Now get the weapons!

(The action shifts back to the captain's cabin. Music begins pulsing in the background.)

TRELAWNEY. I say we load the muskets and mow 'em down!

SMOLLETT. And I say we bide our time for now.

TRELAWNEY. But why?!

SMOLLETT. Because we're outnumbered, three to one at least.

TRELAWNEY. Damn the villains! I'll take three or four of 'em with me!

DR. LIVESY. Captain, do you have a plan?

SMOLLETT. I do. The map of the island shows a stockade and blockhouse just below the North Inlet. If we made it there, we'd stand a better chance.

(BANG! We hear a musket shot from the other camp.)

TRELAWNEY. What's that?!

DR. LIVESY. A gunshot!

SMOLLETT. Quick! Start loading the muskets!

(As LIVESY, TRELAWNEY, SMOLLETT and JIM start pulling muskets out of a chest and loading them, the action shifts to the PIRATES. SILVER, HANDS and BLAND rush in.)

SILVER.

What's goin' on?! Ya arrant lobster-heads!
Ya shiverin' bone-eared kites!
Did I tell ya to stand back and
Hold yer water?! Hanh?!
(BANG! A bullet whistles by the PIRATES, shattering a lamp
next to HANDS'S head.)

SILVER.

Now look what you've done!

HANDS.

That could a' killed me!

(The action shifts back to the captain's cabin. During the
following, we hear shots. The PIRATES have opened
fire on the cabin. Bullets are whizzing by, shattering the
windows, as the four heroes continue loading their muskets
and firing. Smoke is billowing from the rifles and filling the
cabin.)

JIM. Please, sir, I have an idea. I'll go out and speak to
them while the three of you make your escape to the longboat.

TRELAWNEY. What?!

JIM. I got you into this and I'll get you out of it. You see,
it's the map they want and that'll distract them! Then I'll get
away!

SMOLLETT. But how?

JIM. There isn't time to explain. Just take the longboat and
I'll meet you at the stockade.

DR. LIVESY. Don't be absurd. We face it together. ...

Jim!

(But before they can stop him, JIM kicks the door open and rushes out of the room and onto the deck. He carries two loaded pistols with him.)

TRELAWNEY.
Stop!
DR. LIVESY.
Stop!

(The action shifts back to the deck, as JIM emerges from the cabin brandishing the pistols.)

SILVER.
Hold yer fire! HOLD YER FIRE!
(The firing stops.)
Jim! Let's talk! I got a bargain to propose!

(SILVER steps forward – as fearlessly as JIM did – so the two of them can talk face to face and man to man.)

   JIM. Talk all you want! But these pistols are loaded and I know how to use them!
   SILVER. Jim-lad –
   JIM. Don't "Jim-lad" me. And if I ever thought of you in the same...instant as my father, I can only pray that he doesn't know the shame I've brought to his name by doing so.
   SILVER. He was a good man, your father.
   JIM. *Shut up!* ... Now it's the map you want, and I've got it. Right here! See?!

*(He pulls the map out of his jacket and brandishes it. When
    MERRY sees the map, he rushes at JIM and JIM lets off
    one of the pistols – BANG!.)*

MERRY. *Ahh!*... Why you little *punk!*

*(The PIRATES [except for SILVER] start chasing JIM, but he's
    too quick for them. He runs and ducks and runs some more
    – and finally jumps onto the railing of the ship and holds
    the map at arm's length, where it flaps in the wind.)*

JIM.
*I'LL DROP IT! I SWEAR TO GOD I'LL DROP IT OVER THE
SIDE AND YOU'LL NEVER SEE IT AGAIN!
(MERRY grabs a musket and aims it at JIM.)
GO AHEAD AND SHOOT ME! I'LL FALL INTO THE SEA
AND THE MAP'LL GO WITH ME AND THEN WHERE'LL
YOU BE?!!*

    SILVER. What is it ya want, lad? In exchange for the
map?

    DR. LIVESY. *(Off, in the distance.)*
Jim!...Jim!

    JIM. *(Calling)*
Did you make it?!

       SMOLLETT. *(Off)*
We have! We're in the water! We're shoving off!

    JIM. Then I have what I want. And all of you can go to hell
with Captain Flint and all the other pirates who have perished in
your damnable trade.

(And JIM leaps off the railing.
Nay, he soars through the air like a bird, up, high into the air,
with the map in one hand, his pistol in the other. As he
comes down, he disappears from sight and we hear the
splash of his body as it hits the sea. He's made his escape.
The PIRATES rush to the railing to see JIM in the water; and
SILVER smiles, despite himself.)

SILVER. Well done, lad.

END OF ACT ONE

ACT II

Scene 1

(Music. Dissonant and mysterious. The lights come up on Skeleton Island. We're in the inland jungle of trees and vines, mossy fungus and flowering plants. The gnarled boughs of the trees are curiously twisted, and the foliage is compact, like thatch. Snakes and iguanas prosper among the thick undergrowth; and steam from the heat of the day rises like fog from the mossy ground.

Little by little, we see a man, completely still, sitting alone in a small clearing, his legs crossed, his head cocked upward, listening hard to a sound he's just heard. His name is BEN GUNN. He's wiry and emaciated, with a white beard and scraggly white hair, so long and filthy a bird could be nesting there. His clothes are sun-baked rags, patched together from skins and old cloth, hanging off his frame by a thread. His skin has been baked by the sun until it's as brown as a chestnut, and his eyes are rheumy and sad, as though he's lived for at least two lifetimes already.

After a moment, he hears the noise he was listening for: voices and a distant gunshot. Instantly, he scrambles away with the agility and speed of a jungle animal and hides behind the enormous leaf of a giant fern. The offstage noises get progressively louder and the gunshots continue.)

PIRATES. *(Off)*
This way!
I just saw him!
Let's head 'im off!

(Suddenly, JIM HAWKINS races into the clearing like a desperate animal being pursued by wild hounds. He is, indeed, trapped, and he doesn't know where to turn. He looks desperately in both directions – at which moment, BEN GUNN shoots out from behind his leaf and grabs JIM by the wrist.)

JIM.
Ah!
		BEN.
Be quiet!

(BEN pulls JIM behind the fern so that they're both invisible. As they disappear, the PIRATES rush in from different sides, shooting their rifles. They include GEORGE MERRY, JUSTICE DEATH, ANNE BONNY, JOSIAH BLAND and EZEKIEL HAZARD. SILVER stumps in after them.)

SILVER.
STOP! STOP YER SHOOTIN'! He's got ya aimin' at each other, ya fools! You'll be massacree'd without his liftin' a finger!

		BONNY. He's gotta be close by, we saw him!

		SILVER. Ya think ya saw him here and there and everywhere. Well this island's a devil and she'll swallow ya up. And that lad's smarter than all the rest of you mixed together in a thin broth.

(Thump! By this time, BEN has climbed like a monkey to the top of a tree behind the PIRATES and silently hurled a rock so that it lands with a thump far off in the distance.)

BONNY. That'll be him!
DEATH. Hurry up!
HAZARD. Before he gets away!

(The PIRATES run off. BEN watches, to make sure they're gone; then he scampers down the tree and leads JIM out of hiding.)

BEN GUNN. We's outa the woods, we's outa the woods, except, except we's still *in* the woods, now ain't we? Hee, heeeeee!

JIM. ...Who are you?

BEN GUNN. Ben Gunn, says I. Poor Ben Gunn. And I ain't spoke with a Christian these three long years. Or is it four, says I. Can't tell. Mighty hard. Mighty hard.

JIM. Were you shipwrecked?

BEN GUNN. "Shipwrecked"?! Nay, not I. I was *marooned.*

JIM. "Marooned"?

BEN GUNN. Put ashore. Abandoned by a crew o' pirates. And I lives all these years on goats and berries and oysters, and I'll tell you a secret: I's plenty sick o' goats and berries and oysters. Hee, heeeeee! Have an oyster?

(He puts his hand out, offering an oyster.)

JIM. No thank you.

BEN GUNN. What I really wants is a piece o' cheese. *Has you got any on ya?!*

JIM. No. I'm sorry.

BEN GUNN. That was my favorite, see? Cheese, cheese, a little roasted, toasted cheesie, like me mother used to make when I was all tucked up in me little bed at home. Ohh, she was a good soul, me mother. And she loved me, she did. And look at me now, says I. I've been a disappointment, ain't I? That I have. That I have. And all I wants is a piece of cheese.

(He starts to cry.)

JIM.

I'm sorry for your hardship, sir. But there's plenty of cheese on the ship I came on. The one out there.

BEN GUNN. And you'd give me some?

JIM.

Of course I would. I'd be happy to. If I ever get back to it.

BEN GUNN. *Cheese, cheese, cheese! Ha, ha! I's rich!* Ohh, you're a mighty good lad, says I. A fine lad. A magnificent lad! And what's your name?

JIM. Jim Hawkins.

BEN GUNN.

… Jim…Hawkins.

(He looks Jim up and down.)

He heeeeeeeeeee!

(He's delighted about something.)

How dee do, *Jim Hawkins.* Glad to make your acquaintance, lad. And I'll tell ya this. You'll bless your stars that it was you that found me first and was kind to me. Shall I tell ya why? Eh? Hm? Ha ha? Cause I's *rich,* lad. *Rich as the Kings and Queens*

o'Europe ever dreamed of bein' amen and God be with ya! Hee,
hee! And I's built me a little boat, ya see, a magnificent boat, fit
for a king, and I keeps it under the *white rock.* Hee, hee!
Richly riches on the billy goat's hill
Pull ya to the ground if ya don't stand still!
Wait!
(A new thought.)
That ain't Flint's ship out there, is it?

JIM. No sir. Flint is dead, or so they say. But some of
Flint's hands were on board with us, and they mutinied to get a
treasure map. And now I and others loyal to the captain are on
the run.

BEN GUNN. Aha. You're in a clove hitch, ain't ya? Well
you just put your trust in old Ben Gunn. Ben Gunn's the man to
save ya, says I. But tell me, Jim, do ya think your captain dear
would help a poor maroon, if that maroon goes and helps the
captain?

JIM. I would think it likely.

BEN GUNN. To the tune of a passage home …?

JIM. Of course he would! I can promise you!

BEN GUNN.

(Dancing around happily.)
Hee, hee! Hee, hee! I's as good as free!
We'll make for the sea and away from the tree,
For a little fee, on me mother's knee!
Hee, heeeeeeeee!
Now I'll tell you a story and I'll tell ya no more:
I were on Flint's ship when the treasure was buried!
Ya see he orders his first mate, Long John Silver,
To do it and take six of us along
With him to do the work; and he tells Silver,

"You kill 'em afterwards, leavin' no witnesses
Who could point the way!" And Silver says,
"Aye, aye, sir! Aye, aye!" says he,
"I'll *kill* 'em."

    JIM. But why does Silver need the map if he's the one who
buried the treasure?

    BEN GUNN.

Because it's a *jungle* out there, ya silly goose!
With vines and trees and holes and caverns and it
All looks the same to every living soul
In the world! Except to old Ben Gunn, hee heee.
Except to Ben what only wants a piece of cheese.
That's all. That's all I want. That's all I want.

(He weeps again. JIM is moved.)

    JIM. I'm sorry.

(He touches BEN'S shoulder in sympathy – and BEN weeps all
    the harder at the touch of a human after all these years. At
    last BEN looks up.)

    BEN GUNN.

Just look at you. The spittin' image o' your
Darlin' father.

    JIM. *(White)* … My father?

    BEN GUNN.

                                               Peter Hawkins.
Now don't tell old Ben Gunn he ain't your father.
He used to talk about ya night and day
Like you was the greatest livin' creature ever

Made by God.

JIM. How-how did you know my father?

BEN GUNN. We was mates on the ship! The Devil Ship!

JIM. *(Dazed)* But my father never went to sea. He died in London.

BEN GUNN.

Aye, I suppose he would have – if Long John Silver

Hadn't pressed him into service. Ya see,

Flint was about to sail and he needed a cook,

'Cause Silver was now old Flint's first mate.

And Silver'd made a friend o' your father in London Town.

He says "Come along!" and your father says "No,

Not me, I ain't a-goin'." So Silver

Grabs him like and hits him on the head,

And your father wakes up starin' at Orion's Belt,

In the night sky over a bobbin' ship.

JIM. But I received a letter from London, saying that he died!

BEN GUNN.

That'd be from Silver, I'll wager. Hee hee!

He was a dab hand at tyin' up the package.

(He shakes his head sadly.)

Only I'm sorry to say your father was one o' the

Six of us who was told to bury the treasure.

JIM. So then he …?

(Bang! A gunshot.)

BEN GUNN. What's that?! They're comin'! Gotta hide!

JIM. Tell me first what happened!

SMOLLETT. *(Off)*
Jim! Jim, is that you?!
  JIM.
Captain Smollett?!

(CAPTAIN SMOLLETT rushes on.)

  SMOLLETT. Oh thank God! We were worried sick.
  JIM. Where are the others?
  SMOLLETT. They're in the stockade. I was trying to get
the supplies from the boat, but Silver's men just spotted me.

(JIM looks around. BEN is gone.)

  JIM. Where's Ben?
  SMOLLETT. Who?
  JIM. Ben Gunn. He was right here. A man from the jungle
...
  SMOLLETT. Jim, we have to hurry.
  JIM. He had news of my father. I have to talk to him!
  SMOLLETT. Do you still have the map?
  JIM. Yes, it's right here. But I must talk to Ben!

(Bang!)

  SMOLLETT.
Not now you don't. Come on!
  JIM. *I have to!* I'll meet you at the stockade. I promise.

(Bang, bang!)

PIRATES. *(Off)*
There he is! Through the trees!
JIM.
Just go!

(SMOLLETT rushes off in one direction, JIM in the other. As they disappear, the PIRATES rush on.)

PIRATES.
There he is!
I see him!
After him!
SILVER.
Just don't let him get to the stockade!

(The PIRATES rush off after SMOLLETT. Beat. Then JIM RE-ENTERS and addresses the audience.)

JIM. I raced through the dense woods to find Ben Gunn, but the more I searched, the more lost I became. I continued for hours in the desperate hope of learning more about my father, but before I knew it, the sun was setting and I was lost in the ever-increasing darkness of the tangled woods. The next morning I awoke to a gunshot. Within moments, I realized, to my astonishment, that I was on a bluff a mere hundred yards from the stockade. And although I was hidden from view by the trees, I could see and hear everything that was then transpiring in the clearing below.

(We now see the stockade and blockhouse, which includes the fence of the stockade at one side of the stage, then an empty

no-man's-land in the middle, then the blockhouse itself, both inside and out.

As the lights change, LONG JOHN SILVER, holding a white flag, approaches the blockhouse. He's wearing his finest greatcoat, with brass buttons, and a handsome hat. ANNE BONNY and JUSTICE DEATH, armed to the teeth, accompany SILVER from behind.)

SILVER.
Flag o' truce! Flag o' truce! Captain Silver to come aboard and make terms!

(CAPTAIN SMOLLETT comes out of the blockhouse with DR. LIVESY and SQUIRE TRELAWNEY behind him.)

SMOLLETT. "Captain" Silver? Never heard of him. Do you give yourself a promotion so easily?

SILVER. Not I, sir. But these poor lads in my crew have chosen me captain, after your desertion.

SMOLLETT. Desertion?

SILVER. You left the ship, did ya not? And what were my poor boys to do then? It's in their nature to crave a leader – that's how they're constituted – and surely you wouldn't deny 'em their nature. That would be cruelty. Now shall we have a parley?

SMOLLETT. … Come. My men will hold their fire. You have my word.

SILVER. And your so-be-it is good enough for me, one gentleman to another. *(He nods to DEATH and BONNY, who move back.)* Shall we go inside where I can sit meself down and get off this excuse for a leg?

SMOLLETT. No, you'll stay out here. If you had pleased to be an honest man, you might have been sitting in your own galley. You're either my ship's cook, and treated handsomely, or "Captain" Silver, a common mutineer and pirate. Now state your terms.

SILVER. My terms is, we want the treasure, and we'll have it! And *you'd* just as soon save your necks, I reckon. So I believe we have the makin's of a bargain.

SMOLLETT. … Go on.

SILVER. Now you've got a map that I believe shows this island and where the treasure's buried.

SMOLLETT. That's as may be.

SILVER. Well it's my property and I want it back!

SMOLLETT. I thought it was Captain Flint's map.

SILVER. I'm Captain now, so it's mine by law.

SMOLLETT. What law is that?

SILVER. The law of Right and Wrong, or haven't you heard of that one. Lord have mercy, I've got to be careful associating with the likes of you or I'll have me morals corrupted. Now listen, Captain, I never meant you no harm. I'm a peaceful man at heart, a Quaker by nature, and I crave nothin' but the "piping time of peace," as the poet says.

SMOLLETT. I know exactly what you crave and what you meant to do, but I don't care, for now you can't do it.

SILVER. And that's as may be, too, but here's me terms: You hand us the map and I'll give you a choice: Either you come aboard when the treasure's loaded, in which case I give you me word of honour that I'll clap ya some place safe ashore. Or, if that ain't to yer fancy, you can stay here, we'll divide stores, and I'll give ya me affy-davy that I send ya the first ship I sight on the water to come and pick you up. Now handsomer than that you couldn't look for.

    SMOLLETT. Is that all?

    SILVER. Every word. Refuse it and you've seen the last of me but musket balls.

    SMOLLETT. That's quite an offer. Now here's mine. If you'll come up, one by one, unarmed, no tricks, I'll engage to clap you all in irons and take you home to a fair trial in England. If you won't, why, in the name of heaven, I'll put a bullet in your back the next time we meet!

    SILVER.
We'll see who takes the bullet, Captain!
(Calling into the blockhouse.)
Jim! I know you're inside there, lad, now listen! If you join up with us, then all is forgiven. You're too smart to pick the losin' side, so I'll be waitin' for ya in the camp! We're mates, lad, and don't ya forget it!

    SMOLLETT. Get out. *Now!*

    SILVER. With the greatest of pleasure. And I suggest you arm yourself as quick as you can, 'cause I'm comin' back in the grindin' of a tooth and them that die'll be the lucky ones.

(SILVER EXITS like an offended emperor, as SMOLLETT disappears into the blockhouse. As they go, JIM turns to the audience:)

    JIM. The moment I heard Silver's words and saw him stump back to his camp for a hurried conference, I knew that the only place for me was beside my friends, regardless of the odds.

(The action shifts to the inside of the blockhouse, as JIM runs in.)

SMOLLETT. Jim lad!
TRELAWNEY. Well there's the boy!
LIVESY. Jim, thank God you're all right.
JIM. And you, sir.

(Shift to the PIRATES.)

MERRY. Get ready, boys, and we'll attack 'em from the front!

SILVER. Check your powder first and spread out. I'm giving the orders here, George Merry.

(Shift back to the defenders where we see LIVESY and TRELAWNEY loading muskets as SMOLLETT directs operations while still keeping an eye on what's happening outside.)

SMOLLETT. That's it. Keep going, quick as you can.

TRELAWNEY. I'm doing my best. Forgive me if my hand shakes a little, knowing that twenty cutthroat pirates are out there waiting to hack me to pieces.

JIM. I think the attack could be any second now.

TRELAWNEY.
Well why do you think I'm sweating my guts out over this powder and (BANG! A loud shot from the other side of the stockade goes through a window, almost cutting TRELAWNEY down. Ideally, it hits an oil lamp on a table, which then explodes.) Good God!

LIVESY. Hand me a rifle!
SMOLLETT. And for God's sake stay low!

(A volley of shots are fired from behind the stockade — either through chinks in the stockade or by pirates appearing above the top —. SMOLLETT, LIVESY and TRELAWNEY RETURN the fire as JIM, behind them, reloads their firearms as fast as he can. As the shooting continues, we shift our focus back and forth between the PIRATES and the defenders.)

SILVER. Make your shots count! We're low on musket balls!

(In the course of the shooting, SMOLLETT gets shot in the arm.)

JIM.
Mr. Smollett!
LIVESY.
Captain!
SMOLLETT. *(Holding his arm.)* It's all right...Ow! I'm fine, I'm fine! It's only a flesh wound.
TRELAWNEY. Wait a moment. Look! They've stopped coming.
LIVESY. Thank God for that. Did we finish them off, do you think?
SMOLLETT. Impossible. There's too many of them. They're just regrouping.
TRELAWNEY. I'd like to "regroup" them into small pieces.
JIM. *(Offering a rifle.)* Sir, we're out of powder. This is the last one.

LIVESY. Do you think we have a chance against them?

SMOLLETT. I think there might be if one of us could somehow get to the ship and cut the anchor loose. Then she'd drift to the North Inlet and we could make a run for it and try to grab her. Of course they'd chase us all the way.

TRELAWNEY. I'd like to "chase" them to Kingdom Come.

(Shift to the PIRATES.)

SILVER.
Pin 'em down, ya swabs! Don't hang back! Keep the pressure up!

BONNY. The ammunition is gone!

DEATH. And so is the powder!

SILVER.
And do you know what I say to that? Hanh?
I say it's Providence! The Divine Hand
Insurin' that we stand together and fight
Like men of the first water!
To the front, boys! Show me your colors and scale
That wall as though your lives depended on it!

DEATH. The crew has voted that you should go first.

SILVER. And that I will, Master Death, that I will.

(SILVER fires the last round and the PIRATES charge the stockade, swarming over its side.)

LIVESY. Look out! Here they come again!

*(As the PIRATES attack, some are killed as they climb over
    the stockade; some of them make it halfway across the no-
    man's-land; and some of them get as far as the blockhouse,
    thrusting their cutlasses through the wall and firing their
    pistols at close range.*
Suddenly, JIM makes a dash for the door.)

TRELAWNEY. … Jim?
LIVESY.
Jim, where are you going?!
    JIM.
(Calling over his shoulder as he runs.)
I'll be back, I promise!

*(The defenders follow JIM out of the blockhouse and they
    fight the PIRATES at close quarters in the middle of the
    clearing.*
*As the battle continues, JIM appears at the side of the stage and
    addresses the audience.)*

JIM. I ran from the stockade on sheer impulse. I remembered
that Ben Gunn had spoken of a boat he'd constructed, fit for a
king, under a white rock. I ran like a madman along the shore of
the island, praying that my scheme was not in vain…and then I
saw it: *(JIM finds the boat under the rock. At the same time, the
deck of the Hispaniola takes shape in the distance.)* a coracle,
a small boat, patched together by an unskilled hand, yet with
every sign of being seaworthy. Without thinking twice, I leapt
into the craft and paddled furiously for the Hispaniola. Captain
Smollett had said that we might be saved if one of us could cut
the ship from her anchor, and that was now my mission.

Scene 2

(We are now on the deck of the Hispaniola. The deck is empty,
save for two men at a table, playing cards. They are ISRAEL
HANDS and JOB O'BRIEN. They look terrible: shabby,
bored and truculent. They drink heavily as they play. Real
money is at stake.
They play in silence. Then, laying down their hands:)

HANDS. Sixes.
O'BRIEN. Eights.

(O'BRIEN chuckles as he rakes in his winnings.)

HANDS. I's sick o' waitin' things out on this stinkin'
ship.

(O'BRIEN shuffles the deck. Hands watches him. O'BRIEN is
suspiciously adept with the cards...)

HANDS. Lemme see them pasteboards.

(He examines the cards. They seem normal.)

HANDS. Deal.

(O'BRIEN deals in silence. They pick up their cards. Examine
them. The game is like poker. It requires a draw. They
bet. Then:)

HANDS. Two.

(O'BRIEN deals him two.)

    O'BRIEN. Three.

(O'BRIEN deals himself three. They look at their cards. They both put in more money...)

    O'BRIEN. Call.
    HANDS. Eights.
    O'BRIEN. Nines.

(O'BRIEN starts raking in the pot again.)

    HANDS. Hold it! I says you're cheatin'.
    O'BRIEN. Of course I ain't cheatin'. This is relaxation. I'm a pirate. I cheat for a livin'.
    HANDS. Roll up your sleeve.
    O'BRIEN. No.
    HANDS. Roll it up, I say! I says you's a cheater and I wants a look!
    O'BRIEN. And I says you's a poxy bad loser and you're seein' nothin'!
    HANDS. Gimme that arm!
    O'BRIEN. No!
    HANDS. Gimme!
    O'BRIEN. Leggo!
    HANDS. You're a cheat!
    O'BRIEN. You're a liar!

(So quickly we almost miss it, Hands pulls out a knife and plunges it deep into O'BRIEN'S chest.)

O'BRIEN.
AHHHHHHHH!

*(As O'BRIEN falls, he plunges his knife into HANDS'S thigh.
He hits an artery and the wound bleeds profusely.)*

HANDS.
AHHHHHHH!

*(O'BRIEN dies. HANDS is screaming with pain. Then he
collapses, unconscious. We can see the knife sticking out
of his leg.*
Silence. The deck is still.
Then JIM clambers over the side of the ship, dripping wet.)
*He's tired and spent. He's been cutting the hawser. He leans
against the rail to catch his breath…then sees the two men
lying on the deck and gasps.*
*He hurries over to O'BRIEN and winces. He then approaches
the second body, which is face down. He prods it with his
foot. To his surprise, the body groans and rolls over.)*

JIM. Mr. Hands …?
HANDS.
Unnnnh …
    JIM. Mr. Hands, what happened?! O'Brien is dead.
    HANDS. I know. I killed him.
    JIM. Why?
    HANDS. He was too good at cards.

*(He laughs at this – and the laugh turns into a deathly cough.
There's a brandy bottle nearby and JIM hands it to him.)*

JIM. Are you much hurt?

HANDS. If that doctor was aboard, I'd be right enough. But I has no luck. That's what's the matter with me. It's the story of me life.

(JIM pulls the knife out of HANDS'S leg and HANDS screams with pain. As JIM goes to put the knife somewhere safe, the ship lurches, and JIM and HANDS tumble to one side, then the other. Then HANDS realizes what happened.)

HANDS. God's blood! You sliced the bleedin' hawser, didn't ya?!

JIM. And what if I did?

HANDS. Ya brainless lubber, we could drift out to sea!

JIM. I doubt that highly. Captain Smollett says we'll drift to the North Inlet.

HANDS.
Maybe yes and maybe no. *(A sly look crosses HANDS'S face.)* But you'll get there faster if ya sail her yourself, now won't ya? So I got a proposition to make.

JIM. I'm listening.

HANDS. You fetch me somethin' to eat and make it quick and I'll teach you how to sail us into shore like a man.

JIM. To the North Inlet?

HANDS.
What do I care where ya puts her?!
I has no ch'ice, now has I?! Do we have a bargain?!

JIM. … Yes. Take this for your wound.

(JIM gives him his handkerchief. Hands takes it and begins tying his wound up.)

HANDS. Now climb to the wheel and release the lock. *(JIM does as he's told.)* Good. Now give her a spin to starboard. Ya see how the topsail's fillin' up? Like the belly of a woman bustin' out with a whelp. That's what you want.

(JIM stands at the wheel, proud of his new-found abilities. Meanwhile, HANDS is forming his own plans and has to hide a smile.)

HANDS. You'll want to leave her now for a while – and I wants me grub.

JIM. There's some food left right over here.

HANDS. *Well I can't move, now can I?!* And I want some, uh ... *wine.* This brandy's too strong. And I want some beef and biscuits. You'll have to go below. *Now that's our bargain!*

JIM. You'll get what I can find quickly and nothing more. I'll be right back.

(JIM walks quickly away and disappears down the hatch. When HANDS is sure that JIM is out of sight, he tries to get to his feet. The wound burns with pain, but he manages to stand up; then he hobbles forward, limping badly.
He makes it to O'BRIEN'S body – and pulls the knife out of O'BRIEN'S chest. It's an evil-looking dirk with a curved, wicked blade. HANDS looks around to make sure that JIM hasn't come back, and he hides the knife in the belt of his pants, making sure that it's covered by his shirt. Then he hobbles quickly back to where he started and assumes the pose he had before JIM left.
Within a beat, JIM appears, bounding up the stairs of the hatch, his arms filled with provisions.)

JIM. I found some *cheese! Ha, ha!* Here, this is for you.

(He gives HANDS the wine and biscuits.)

HANDS. Ya likes cheese, do ya?

JIM. It would appear so, wouldn't it? But things aren't always what they seem, now are they?

(Proud of his double meaning, JIM puts the cheese in his pocket for safe keeping.)

HANDS. You need to get back to the tiller now and hold fast. And ya see them stays? You'll have to release 'em pretty quick in a minute.

JIM. What for?

HANDS. Cause if they're too tight, the sails won't shift! I'd have done it meself, but I can't take a walk with this blasted wound o' mine, now can I? It's keepin' me from movin' a'tall.

(And let it be said that Hands is a pretty terrible liar. Indeed, JIM is now alert to something, but he doesn't know what it is. Warily, but trying to hide his suspicions, JIM moves to the tiller. He has his back to HANDS...and HANDS now gets to his feet and pulls out the knife. He approaches JIM, as quietly as he can.

JIM would later recount what happened next in a book called <u>Treasure Island</u>: *"Perhaps I had heard a creak, or seen his shadow moving with the tail of my eye; perhaps it was an instinct like a cat's; but, sure enough, when I looked around, there was HANDS, already half-way towards me, with the dirk in his right hand. We must both have cried*

*out aloud when our eyes met; but while mine was the shrill
cry of terror, his was a roar of fury like a charging bull's.
At the same instant he threw himself forward, and I leapt
sideways towards the bows. As I did so, I left hold of the
tiller, which sprang sharp to leeward; and I think this saved
my life, for it struck HANDS across the chest, and stopped
him, for the moment, dead."*
*But HANDS isn't dead, and as he stirs, JIM sees him, runs to the
other end of the deck and pulls out one of his pistols.)*

JIM.
*One more step, Mr. Hands, and I'll blow your brains out! I
swear to Heaven I'll do it, so don't try me!!*

*(He takes aim and fires...but there follows neither flash nor
sound. Then he tries the other pistol and it's the same thing.
They've both misfired.)*

HANDS. Wet from the sea, ya lubber. Ha!

*(A tremendous chase ensues: HANDS, his grizzled hair tumbling
over his face, moves fast despite his bleeding thigh; JIM
dodges him at every turn, crying out as the crazed pirate
tries to bury his dirk in the boy's body. Finally, when JIM
appears to be cornered, he springs into the mizzen shrouds.
Quickly, he climbs upward, hand over hand.)*

HANDS.
I's comin' after ya, boy!

(HANDS puts the knife between his teeth and starts to climb. As he does, JIM reaches the cross-trees and sits – then madly begins priming his pistol anew with a fresh ball and shot.)

JIM. *(To himself.)* Come on, come on …
HANDS. You'll never make it!

(With a cry of joy, JIM finishes loading the pistol, and he points it straight down at HANDS, who has almost made it to JIM'S foot.
HANDS stares up at JIM with frustration and rage. Then he takes the knife from between his teeth and with a sudden, unexpected snap, he throws the dirk straight at JIM.)

JIM.
Ahhhh!

(JIM'S pistol goes off with a loud report and HANDS cries out with a shriek of agony. The bullet has hit HANDS in the chest. He sways for a moment, then plunges, with a final cry, into the sea below.
We now see that the knife thrown by HANDS is pinning JIM'S shoulder to the mast. It has only caught the skin and the shirt, but there's blood everywhere, and JIM is in agony. With enormous effort, he pulls the knife out of the mast, releasing his shoulder. The pain is horrid, and he drops the knife onto the deck below. Then he leans against the mast and closes his eyes, half-fainting, but safe at last.)

JIM. *(To the audience.)* Knowing that I'd killed a man, I began to feel faint, and even more terrified than when the danger had been upon me. The thought of it sickened me, yet I knew that defending myself in a man's world had somehow altered me, as though I'd climbed a fence and crossed from a field of flowers to a darker stand of tall but uneven trees. By this time, the *Hispaniola* had run aground in the North Inlet. I waded to shore without much difficulty, and it did not take long after that to find the stockade where my friends would be waiting.

Scene 3

(The action now shifts to the interior of the blockhouse. We can see the outlines of men sleeping in the darkness, presumably DR. LIVESY, SQUIRE TRELAWNEY and CAPTAIN SMOLLETT, and we can hear them snoring. JIM approaches the blockhouse and taps on the door. He gets no response, taps again, then moves quietly into the room.)

JIM. Hello …?

(Silence. Then suddenly, in the darkness, a voice squawks "Pieces of eight! Pieces of eight!" Immediately, the sleepers spring up and a torch is lit, showing a circle of villainous, leering faces in the yellow light. These are not JIM'S friends; these are THE PIRATES – GEORGE MERRY, ANNE BONNY, EZEKIEL HAZARD, JUSTICE DEATH and JOSIAH BLAND – and suddenly JIM can't breathe. From behind the men, SILVER appears.)

SILVER. Well, well, Jim. So you've dropped in on us, have ya? Now I bear that as friendly, I do.
(The PIRATES laugh.)

DEATH. Friendly it is!

BONNY. Right neighborly, I'd say!

(More laughter. To JIM'S ears, it is the laughter of demons.)

SILVER. I take it from your expression that we ain't the flesh and blood you expected to find here tonight.

JIM. No. You're not. *(More laughter from the PIRATES.)* Where are my friends?

SILVER. Now that's a fair question and deserves an answer. And you know I've always liked you, Jim, as a lad of spirit and the very picture of me own self when I were young and innocent.

"What we changed

Was innocence for innocence: we knew not

The doctrine of ill-doing, nor dreamed

That any did."

JIM.

Where are my friends?!

SILVER. They came to us last evening with a flag o' truce. "Captain Silver," says the doctor, "you're sold out. Your men are getting sick from the climate, you're out of stores and your ship is gone." "Gone?" says I. Well, I turn around to look and by thunder! – the ship ain't to be seen! It's a sea o' glass out there, without a wrinkle in it. So then we bargained, givin' them their freedom in exchange for all o' this luxury. But I'm pained to tell ya, boy: I don't think they much appreciated your desertion of 'em. They took it as cowardly.

JIM. Cowardly?!

SILVER. I'm afraid so. And I have to confess, I thought it was too.

JIM. *(Shaking with anger.) You* thought so?! *You?!* The man who kidnapped my father?! The man who trapped him on a ship against his will?! The man who put him to *death* because you didn't dare stand up to Captain Flint?! *(WHAP! JIM slaps SILVER across the face as hard as he can.) There's* for your "cowardly." And *there!* (*WHAP!*) And *there!* (*WHAP!*)

(SILVER hasn't flinched at any of these blows. When JIM is finished, SILVER rubs his cheek and stares at JIM.)

SILVER. If I'd had a son like you, Jim, I can only dream o' the things we might a' done together. But I'll tell ya what. You've got a choice, Jim. Join up with us and take your share as a gentleman o' fortune, or say no and you walks out that door as free as a bird. It's up to you.

JIM. I know what kind of choices you offer. I saw what you did on the ship to Tom Morgan when he said no.

(The PIRATES murmur in astonishment.)

HAZARD. How'd he know that?

BONNY. Who told him …?

JIM. So let the worst come to the worst, it's little I care. I've seen too many perish since I fell in with you. But there's one thing I'll tell you before I die: You're in a bad way. The ship's lost, the treasure's lost, men lost; your whole business has gone to wreck; and if you want to know who did it – *it was I!!* *I* was in the apple barrel and told the captain what I heard! *I* cut the ship's cable and brought her where you'll never see her again. *I* killed Mr. Hands and stopped him from saving the ship for you. And *I* know where the treasure is and you'll never find it, not in a thousand years!

MERRY. *(Pulling his sword.)* You'll die for this, you little maggot!

SILVER. Avast there, George Merry! I'll teach you who's in charge o' this ship!

(SILVER pulls his cutlass and defends JIM. SILVER and MERRY fight with fury, and JIM would surely die if SILVER didn't defend him. In the end, SILVER knocks the sword from MERRY'S hand. MERRY stands panting, eyeing it on the ground nearby. He wants to make a grab for the sword, but he's afraid to.)

SILVER. Go ahead! Make a move! And if ya do, I'll see the color of your insides before ya take another breath! This boy is worth more than all of you jackals put together. Touch a hair on his head and you'll answer to me! *Is that understood?!*

(The crew murmurs assent...but they glance at each other and exchange an understanding.)

HAZARD. This crew has a right to talk, now don't it?

BONNY. We claims the right to step outside for a council.

DEATH. We don't vally bullyin' a marlin-spike, and we aims to talk about it.

HAZARD. Them's the rules and you can't deny it.

SILVER. I deny nothing. Talk is free and liberty is generous.

(The PIRATES file out of the blockhouse. MERRY, before he

*leaves, picks up his cutlass and gives SILVER a look of
defiance that could cut through glass. Then he goes, leaving
SILVER and JIM alone.)*

SILVER. *(With urgency, keeping his voice down.)* Listen to
me, lad. You're within half a plank o' death, and, what's worse,
of torture. They're going to throw me off, that's for certain. But
I'll stand by ya, and you stand by me. Now I got one more string
to me bow, but if it ain't the thing, we'll face 'em back-to-back,
and if it goes hard, we go down together.

JIM. *(Through gritted teeth.)* Do you really think I'd stand
by any man that *killed my father?!*

*(He starts to slap SILVER as he did before, but SILVER catches
his arm and stops him.)*

SILVER. Now don't start that again, me cheek can't take
it.

JIM. You murderer –
SILVER. Jim –
JIM. *Scum!*
SILVER. *Jim – !*
JIM. *You lying, filthy –*
SILVER. *I saved your father's life!!*…Yes, Flint ordered
me to kill your father. And yes, I took him into this blasted
jungle! But after that I set him free – him and an old dog named
…Ben Gunn. *(This startles JIM. Could SILVER be telling the
truth?)* I killed the other four, who'd a' killed me if I hadn't, and
I returned to Flint and said I'd killed all six of 'em, which was
takin' a poxy chance with me life, I'll tell ya that. But I couldn't
kill your father, Jim. We was mates! He was my friend! *(Beat.)*

You know I'm tellin' you the truth. You can see it in me eyes.

    JIM. ...Do you think my father...*(He's overcome.)* Do you think my father might still be alive?

    SILVER. He's not, Jim. Before we sailed he made a break for the ship and Flint cut him down. I had hell to pay from Flint, I promise you. But it was here or London, and he died like a man.

    JIM. Noooo!

(JIM cries. SILVER holds him. Then SILVER hears a noise outside.)

    SILVER. Here come the crows and it's now or never. Are you with me, Jim?

    JIM. ... I'm with you. And I think you'd better keep this.

(JIM hands SILVER the treasure map.)

    SILVER. Are you certain, lad?

    JIM. I am.

    SILVER. Give me your wrists.

(SILVER binds JIM'S hands with a rope with a long lead. A moment later, the PIRATES re-enter. Nervously, they push ANNE BONNY forward.)

    BONNY. Cap'n. I've got somethin' for ya...

    SILVER. Anne Bonny. Me old mate. Come forward, lass, I ain't gonna eat ya. Hand it over. *(She hands him a piece of paper.)* The black spot. I was expectin' that. *(He turns it over.)* Now wait a second. Look'ee here. This ain't scissored out of a Bible, is it? *(The men look at each other, worried.)* This here's *Revelations* on the back! *(Reads, declaiming:)* "And the Lord saith unto me, 'I cannot bear these *evil men.*'" Well, that's rather apt, now ain't it.

MERRY. That's not the point!

SILVER. No, it isn't. But I wouldn't care to be the fool that cut up a Bible! *(EZEKIEL HAZARD starts.)* Was it you, Ezekiel?

HAZARD. We needed paper! There ain't no harm in that! *(Worried:)* Is there, John?

SILVER. Honestly? You're as good as dead.

MERRY. It's a lie!

HAZARD. *You told me to do it, George Merry! And I didn't want to!*

MERRY. *He's tryin' to scare ya! And it ain't the point! (To SILVER.)* The point is, you've got the spot, John Silver. Now read what it says. The part in charcoal!

SILVER. "Deposed." "D-e-p-p-o-s-s-e-d." Is that your hand, George? You've become quite a leader o' this crew, now ain't ya? And by the rules, it's time for me to hear your grievances. Now out with 'em.

MERRY. I'll speak for the crew.

SILVER. What a surprise.

MERRY. *First,* you made a hash o' this cruise – you'd be a bold man to say no to that. *Second*, you let the enemy out o' this here trap for nothin'. *Third*, there's this here boy. He's the devil and you been protectin' him like his old mother. I say we kill him now and be done with it. And *number four, we ain't got the treasure, and we ain't got the bloomin' map!*

(The other PIRATES chime in: "Hear, hear!" "He's right!"

"We wants the gold!"
SILVER takes them all in.)

SILVER. Point one, there'd a' been no cruise if it warn't for me. And if you'd a-waited, like I told ya, there'd be treasure on the ship right now and we'd be sailin' home as smooth as butter. Point two, we needed the stores in this here blockhouse or we'd a' starved to death. Point three, this boy is a *hostage*, ya ninny. Do ya have no *brains?!* Do you have no *sense?!* If the time comes and we need to bargain, he'll be worth his weight in gold! He could save our lives! And point four...*THERE!*

(With a grand gesture, SILVER pulls the treasure map out of his jacket and flings it defiantly on the ground in front of the PIRATES. They gape in awe.)

SILVER. *There's your map!* And if you don't trust old John Silver now, then elect yourselves another leader.

(The PIRATES pick up the map and crowd around it.)

BONNY. It *is* the map!
DEATH. There's Spy-Glass Hill!
BONNY. And here's the crosses!
MERRY. But what about the ship? Even if we track the treasure, how do we get out o' here?
SILVER. We *find* the ship, you codfish, that's how. If the lad cut the hawser, she'll drift ashore. We'll cover every square inch o' the coast until we find her, and find her we will, I'll stake me life on it!
BONNY. Three ...cheers ... *for Captain Silver! Hip-hip*

PIRATES. *Hooray!*
BONNY. *Hip-hip*
PIRATES. *Hooray!*
BONNY. *Hip-hip*
PIRATES. *Hooray!*

(The PIRATES welcome SILVER back into the fold with much back-slapping and revelry. As they do, JIM steps forward.)

JIM. No one closed an eye that night, as the pirates prepared for their assault on the island – and Heaven knows I had matter enough for thought: in the man whom I had slain that afternoon; in my own most perilous position; and in the remarkable game that I saw Silver now engaged upon. But most of all, I thought upon my beloved father and I wept for him.

Scene 4

(We're now in the jungle, early the next morning. Music plays, building the suspense. The sun is blazing down from a white sky; and the earth is hot and steaming. We hear the PIRATES singing; then we see them, armed to the teeth and carrying pickaxes and shovels. They're led by GEORGE MERRY, who holds the map. He's followed by JUSTICE DEATH, ANNE BONNY, EZEKIEL HAZARD and CALICO JACK. Bringing up the rear are LONG JOHN SILVER and JIM HAWKINS. JIM is tethered round the waist with a rope, and the loose end is held by SILVER. They've been on foot in the jungle for over two hours by now, and they're hot, tired and unhappy.)
DEATH. It's hot as the hinges o' hell out here.

BONNY. It's called a swamp, you ninny.

MERRY. *(Reading the map.)* "Three trees in a row, Spy-Glass Shoulder, bearing one point to the north of North-Northeast …"

HAZARD. There they are! Three trees in a row!

DEATH. That's not them. They're gonna be large trees, you idiot.

BONNY. Well that one's large.

DEATH. And the other two is little scrubs.

HAZARD. I think it's this way.

MERRY. *(Using the compass.)* One point north of North-Northeast…

SILVER. *For the love of Abraham, can't you numbskulls read a map?! (He snatches it from MERRY.)* If we get anywhere close, I'll recognize it!

(SILVER walks to one side, leading JIM with him. As he studies the map and speaks quietly to JIM, the other PIRATES – all disgruntled – have a private conference:)

DEATH. I'm gettin' mighty tired o' "dolts" and "numbskulls" …

HAZARD. You'd think he was the King o' Siam or somethin'.

BONNY. I hope he falls down a hole and kills hisself. With a stake through his 'art!

MERRY. And maybe that contingency can be arranged …

HAZARD. What are ya sayin'?

MERRY. I'm saying that when the treasure's found, we

finish him off, once and for all. Death here and Jack can take his arms from behind, Bonny his leg, Hazard his head, and I'll cut his throat, neat as a pie. Are ya with me?

DEATH. ... Aye.

BONNY. Aye.

CALICO JACK. Aye!

HAZARD. He deserves it. If nothin' else, for draggin' us across this horrible island. It's like one big swamp. And when I gets back to civvy-lization, I'm gonna *YAAAAAAAAAAAAAAAH!*

CALICO JACK.
What is it?!

DEATH.
                    What?!

BONNY.
                         What?!

SILVER.
                                   What happened?!

HAZARD.
                                        Look!... *Look!*

(We now see A SKELETON. It's laid out on the ground, the arms straight above the head, bound at the wrists, so it's all in a very straight line. Note: from this point on, the jungle seems to get denser and darker; it closes in on the PIRATES subtly and ominously.)

DEATH. It's unnatural.

BONNY. It's grotesque-like!

HAZARD. What sort o' way is that fer bones to lie?

SILVER. Get the compass and give us a bearing on the way he's pointing.

MERRY. One point to the north o' North-Northeast.

SILVER. He's a marker, pointin' us the way to the treasure.

DEATH. But how – ?

SILVER. Old Flint's idea of a joke.

HAZARD. The savage.

BONNY. Thank God Flint's dead.

DEATH. Aye, aye to that.

CALICO JACK. Here, here!

(Beat. Then a thought strikes all of them at the same time.)

DEATH. … We are pretty sure he's dead, ain't we?

MERRY. We saw him take a cutlass to the back.

HAZARD. I saw it meself with these here deadlights.

BONNY. Aye, but if ever a spirit walked, it would be Flint's. He died so bad.

HAZARD. And he only knew one song in his whole life, remember that? Ha ha!
(Singing; mocking, trying to cheer himself up.)
"FIFTEEN MEN ON A DEAD MAN'S CHEST,
YO HO HO AND A BOTTLE O' RUM –"

A VOICE FROM THE FOREST.
"Drink and the devil had done for the rest,
Yo ho ho and a bottle o' *rummmmmm!*"

(The voice screeches the last word and the sound echoes through

the forest.
Silence. The PIRATES are frozen.)

BONNY.
Lord a-mercy.
    DEATH.
        It's Flint.
    CALICO JACK.
              Flint.

BONNY.
                  It's Flint!

VOICE.
Hee heeeeeeeeeeeeeeeeeeeeeeeeeeeeeeeee!

(Silence.)

DEATH.
Wait a second. ...Where's Jack?
    BONNY.
        What?

DEATH.
            Calico Jack. Our shipmate.

MERRY.
I just saw him.
    BONNY.
      He was right here. I was talkin' to him!
    DEATH.
Well he ain't here now.
Jack where are ya!

    BONNY.

AHHHHHH!

(BONNY has just lifted one of the giant leaves – and there is CALICO JACK, lying on his back with a knife in his chest.)

MERRY.
God have mercy!
  BONNY.

      He's dead.

 DEATH.

          Dead.

 BONNY.

            Who's out there?!

 THE VOICE IN THE FOREST.
Hee heeeeee!
(Singing)
"ALL HAIL TO THE RUM,
ALL HAIL TO THE DRINK,
OLD DARBY MCGRAW
ENDS UP IN THE CLINK."

 MERRY.
WHO ARE YOU?!!
 DEATH. Well whoever he is, he's gonna stop laughin' when I get through with him! Stand back!
(JUSTICE DEATH pulls his sword and disappears boldly into the underbrush. We only hear his voice now, from offstage:)
Where are ya?! Where are ya, I say?! As soon as I find ya, I'm gonna run ya AHHHHHHHHHHHHHHHHHHHHHHHHHH!
(The PIRATES gasp, frozen. Then JUSTICE'S head rolls out of

*the forest and the PIRATES jump back. HAZARD picks up
the head and gapes at it.)*

MERRY. He's dead!

HAZARD. *(Falling to his knees and babbling:)* The Lord
is my shepherd I shall not want he maketh me to lie down in
green pastures he leadeth me beside the still waters he restoreth
my soul –

BONNY. *(Walking off.)* You can pray all ya like, I'm leavin'
here *right now*.

HAZARD. Ya can't! There's somethin' out there!

MERRY. *Wait!* I know what to do…*Come here, you!*

*(MERRY grabs JIM in a powerful lock under the chin and holds
his dirk to JIM'S throat.)*

JIM. *Ah!*

SILVER. *Hey!*

MERRY. *Get back! I'll kill him! I swear to God I'll cut
his throat!*

SILVER. *(Advancing)* George Merry…

MERRY. *Get back, John! I'll do it!*

(SILVER stops – and MERRY calls out as loud as he can:)

MERRY.
*ALL RIGHT!
WHOEVER'S OUT THERE!
LIVESY! TRELAWNEY! SMOLLETT!
SHOW YERSELF OR I KILL THE BOY!
NOW!*

I'LL GIVE YA TO THE COUNT O' THREE.

(He tightens his hold on JIM.)

> **JIM.** *Ah!*
> **MERRY.** *Shut up! (He calls out:) ONE –*

(BANG! A shot rings out, and MERRY falls to the ground with a bullet in his forehead.
Suddenly, with a cry, BEN GUNN jumps out of the jungle, dropping his rifle, and wrestles SILVER to the ground. In an instant, he has the better of SILVER and he's strangling him to death.)

> **SILVER.** *Argh ...! Argh ...!*
> **JIM.** *No! Ben! Stop it!*
> **BEN.** *You left me for dead on this godforsaken island!*
> **SILVER.** *Argh!*
> **JIM.**
BEN! PLEASE! HE SAVED MY LIFE!

(BEN pauses for a moment, breathing hard...then lets SILVER go.)

> **SILVER.** *(Getting up.)* You almost killed me.
> **BEN.** You condemned me to this land of goats and oysters.
> **SILVER.** If you'll remember, Ben, I spared your life.
> **BEN.** *I told you not to listen to Flint!*
> **SILVER.** The good and the bad, Ben, the good and the bad. Sometimes it's pretty hard to separate 'em.

(Out of the woods come DR. LIVESY, SQUIRE TRELAWNEY and CAPTAIN SMOLLETT. TRELAWNEY is carrying two buckets full of jewels. Note: by this time, ANNE BONNY and EZEKIEL HAZARD have made their getaway.)

DR. LIVESY. Jim!

TRELAWNEY. Ha, ha!

CAPTAIN SMOLLETT. Hello, Jim! You look right enough.

JIM. I'm … fine. Wait. Ben. This is for you.

(JIM pulls out the cheese he found aboard the ship and hands it to BEN.)

BEN. …Cheese?

(JIM nods. BEN takes it. And holds it. And weeps.)

JIM. Captain, Squire, have you met Ben yet?

TRELAWNEY. *(In high spirits.)* Met him? Hah! Why we're old friends already, now ain't we, Ben? Eh? Haha? We spot him in the jungle, we how d'ee do, he how d'ee do's back, we offer him safe passage home and he takes us straight to the *treasure.*

JIM. The treasure?

BEN. I dug it up, ya see, four years ago, and hid it in me little cave. Hee heee!

LIVESY. Wait till you see it, Jim.

SMOLLETT. It's quite remarkable.

TRELAWNEY.

(Showing the jewels and putting on a necklace or two.)
"Remarkable?" That is a word, sir, and this is
Triumph Unleashed! Olympus Acquired! Nay,
A Paradise unparalleled and better
Than I ever dreamed! With rows and rows
Of gold and silver and trinkets and jewels
And diamonds and emeralds and jade ha haaa!

*(And as he says it, the back of the stage begins to glow as though
we're now somehow in the cave itself.)*

TRELAWNEY.

(Singing and dancing a jig.)
*"THERE WAS A YOUNG LAD ON THE SEA, THE SEA
THERE WAS A YOUNG LAD ON THE SEAAAAA!"
AND HE DREAMED OF HIS LASSIE, HE DREAMED OF HIS
HOME,
BUT MOSTLY HE DREAMED OF THE SEA, THE SEA,
MOSTLY HE DREAMED OF THE SEA!"*

*(As SQUIRE TRELAWNEY continues to sing and slap the backs
of his companions, they all start to fade into the distance.
As they do, JIM steps forward and addresses the audience.
And now the background changes again, this time into a
vast panorama of the sea.)*

JIM. It took almost four days to load all of the treasure onto
the ship. I had never seen such riches, nor, I'm sure, had the
Kings and Queens of Europe, as Ben liked to call them. On the
fifth day we set sail and maneuvered our way out of the North

Inlet. Coming through the narrows, we had to lie near to the southern point, and there we saw the last two pirates together on a spit of sand, their arms raised in supplication. It went to all our hearts, I think, to leave them in that wretched state; but we could not risk another mutiny, and to take them home for the hangman would have been a cruel sort of kindness. Long John Silver, on the other hand, seemed as cheerful as when I'd first met him and seemed to have not a care in the world for the gallows he would undoubtedly have to face on our return to England. *(The background darkens now, and a room takes shape.)* Captain Smollett, however, clapped him in irons for the last three days of our voyage, keeping him below decks in a makeshift prison fashioned from his old galley. It was there I visited Silver on the morning of the day we sighted land.

Scene 5

(The action shifts to the old galley, now in shadows.
SILVER is alone, chained to the stove but able to move about.
He is in good spirits. JIM feels awkward and bereft.)

SILVER. Well avast ye, Jim. How neighborly of ya to come and visit. And how've ya been keepin', eh? Pleased to be gettin' home, I'll wager.

JIM. Yes. I am. Thank you. I hope you haven't been too uncomfortable. I begged Captain Smollett not to put you here.

SILVER.
Not at all, not at all.
A little solitude is good for a man.
Gives him a chance to contemplate, think,
Plan for the future, and dwell upon his sins

And his virtues. Pull up a chair and put yer feet up
And tell me the news o' the world outside me little room.
For God's sake, let us sit upon the ground,
And tell sad stories of the death o' kings.
For within the hollow crown
That rounds the mortal temples of a king
Keeps Death his court;
    JIM.
And there the antic sits
Scoffing his state and grinning at his pomp,
    SILVER.
As if this flesh which walls about our life
    BOTH.
Were brass impregnable.

    SILVER. Very good, Jim! Excellent! Excellent!
    JIM. *(Distressed)*
How-how can you be so cheerful! You could face the gallows!

    SILVER. I could. Aye. But then again they might just pat
me on the head and let me off for good behavior. That's why
it's all so much fun, Jim. Part o' life's rich tapestry.

(JIM wipes away a tear that he didn't want SILVER to see. He
knows that he'll never set eyes on SILVER again.)

    SILVER. Now come on, boy. Always look to the front.
Never look back. It slows ya down.
    JIM. ... I've brought you a present.
    SILVER. Oooh, let's see, let's see. I love presents. Me
birthday is me favorite national holiday. Ha!
(JIM pulls a large key out of his pocket and holds it up.)

SILVER. No!
JIM. I'm afraid so.

(JIM starts unlocking SILVER'S restraints, setting him free.)

SILVER. Why, Jim, you scoundrel! Ha haaa! *(Rubbing his wrists.)* But you could get into a lot o' trouble for this. They could put you in jail. Honest.

JIM. They could. And wouldn't that be part of *my* rich tapestry…*(SILVER laughs.)* We'll be getting into port in about ten minutes. You still have time to slip over the railing.

SILVER. You, uh…you wouldn't think it possible, I suppose, to send me off like with a bit o' that…bounty that's goin' to waste in the hold nearby. It's not for meself, mind; it's for *your* benefit – to try and lessen the burden that too much capital might have on a young lad like yourself.

(JIM gives him a look … then pulls out two sacks of coins that he's been hiding under his shirt. SILVER laughs happily and takes them.)

SILVER. Ah, Jim, what a son you'd a made.

("Oweeeeeeeeeeeeeeee!")

BEN GUNN. *(Off)* Comin' into port!
CAPTAIN SMOLLETT. *(Off)* All hands on deck!
SILVER. I'd better hurry lad. Take good care.

JIM. Wait! Don't forget Captain Flint. *(The parrot.)*
SILVER. He's for you, Jim. To remember me by.

(Jim is speechless. They embrace. And SILVER goes.)

JIM. *(To the audience.)*...That was the last I ever saw of the seafaring man with one leg that Billy Bones first warned me of. And once again I dream about him, this time standing on the prow of a ship, looking out towards the horizon, smiling at whatever the future might happen to bring. And then I know that my adventure on Treasure Island didn't end that morning on the Hispaniola – and that it will never end as long as I live.

(The lights fade.)

CURTAIN

PROPERTY LIST

6' DIAMETER FAN
WASH TUB
SR AND SL RAMPS
3 ROLLING PANELS
GIANT MAP
SAILS
ROPE SAILS
ARMCHAIR
STOOL
RUM BOTTLE
FLINT'S PAPER BIRD
BREAKABLE BOARD IN PANEL
BIBLE W/ TORN BLACK SPOT PAGE
BRASS TELESCOPE
BIG CHEST
JACKET AND HAT
FLYING MAP
BARREL
TABLE TOPPER
SM. TABLE
RAG
APRON
4 TANKARDS
RUM BOTTLE
BLACK BIRDCAGE
CRATE
BROOM
BLONDE STOOL
SUITCASE

3 LARGE BUNDLES
2 SM. BUNDLES
4 BUCKETS
BRANDY BOTTLE
JIM'S ROPE
DISTRESSED UNION JACK
RUBBER RIFLE
CHAINS
CHAIN BUCKET
CUPS
WATER PITCHER
THROAT LOZENGES
SAFETY PINS
TISSUES
TRASH CAN
2 BUCKETS
STOVE
COFFEE POT
4 POTATOES
2 POTS
FAKE POTATOES ON BOX
CANNON
RIFLE RACK
2 SM. KEGS
BEGGAR CART
WEAPON RACK
WEAPON CABINETS
BLUE MAT
TRESTLE TABLE
4 STOOLS
TRESTLE TABLE

CHAIR, BLONDE STOOL, BROWN STOOL
APPLE BARREL
BROKEN PEW GLASSES
3 TANKARDS
LARGE SILVER TRAY
1 COIN
TOWEL
BIBLE
2 COINS
HANDKERCHIEF
5 POSTERS
PARROT IN CAGE
BUCKET
BUCKET W/ BRUSH
BROOM
OAR
DISTRESSED UNION JACK
FLAG OF TRUCE
BLOODY MAP
3 PLAYING CARDS
GUNPOWDER SATCHEL
2 COINS
2 BUCKETS OF TREASURE
KEY
SACK OF GOLD
DEATH'S HEAD
HAND BARROW
SEAMANS CHEST
CLOTHING
MAP
KILLER CART

3 KEGS
CUPS
WATER PITCHER
THROAT LOZENGES
SAFETY PINS
TISSUES
TRASH CAN
HELM
BRASS TELESCOPE
2 STOOLS
SAILBOAT
LANTERN
PIECE OF CHEESE
BOTTLE OF WINE
CUPS
WATER PITCHER
THROAT LOZENGES
SAFETY PINS
TISSUES
TRASH CAN
BROWN NET
SKELETON
POSTER MAP
LETTER
SHAKESPEARE BOOK
BROWN SATCHEL
BLACK SPOT
BLACK SPOT ON STRING
BIG BRASS KEY

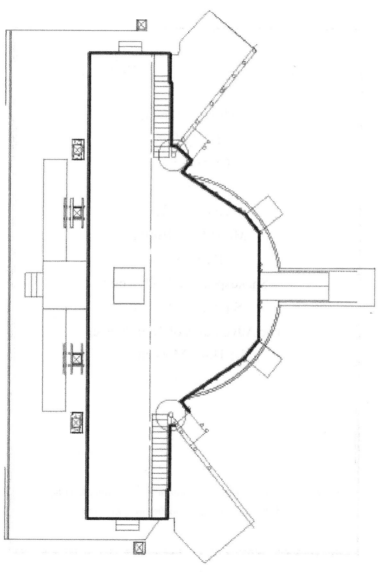

SET DESIGN

Also by Ken Ludwig...

The Beaux' Stratagem

Be My Baby

Crazy for You

Leading Ladies

Lend Me a Tenor

Moon Over Buffalo

Postmortem

Shakespeare in Hollywood

Sullivan & Gilbert

The Adventures of Tom Sawyer

The Three Musketeers

Twentieth Century

*Please visit our website www.samuelfrench.com for complete
descriptions and licensing information*